Watkin swept up the rifle, drawing back the hammer at the same time. Kit reached for the pistol in his belt only to discover that he'd lost it somewhere in the struggle. Grabbing the tomahawk from his waist, Kit swung out, connecting with the rifle's barrel and knocking it aside just as Watkin's finger was closing on the trigger.

The rifle exploded near Kit's ear with racking pain.

Watkin was quick. He reversed the rifle, grabbed the barrel, hauled back and took a swipe at Kit's head. If it had connected he'd have split it open like a ripe pumpkin. But Kit was just as quick. His tomahawk rang out against the steel butt plate. The rifle whirled around again, this time catching the short ax by its head and knocking it from Kit's fist.

Kit had only his butcher knife left.

Other books in the *Kit Carson* series:
#1: THE COLONEL'S DAUGHTER
#2: GHOSTS OF LODORE
#3: REDCOAT RENEGADES

KIT CARSON

KEELBOAT CARNAGE

DOUG HAWKINS

LEISURE BOOKS NEW YORK CITY

For Don D'Auria

A LEISURE BOOK®

July 1998

Published by

Dorchester Publishing Co., Inc.
276 Fifth Avenue
New York, NY 10001

ISBN 0-8439-4411-0

Printed in the United States of America.

ACKNOWLEDGMENTS

My sincerest thanks to the late Dr. Thomas Edward, who so graciously allowed me to roam freely through his rare and valuable collection of monographs by that nineteenth-century Native American scholar, Professor W. G. F. Smith.

KEELBOAT CARNAGE

Chapter One

"You want what?" Rafe Smitter roared, taking a menacing step forward.

From all around them came the soft rattle of weapons coming to bear.

At Smitter's side, Jimmy Watkin put out a hand and stopped his partner. "You better settle down, Rafe," Watkin said beneath his breath, smiling genially at the forty Blackfoot warriors standing before them. "Let me handle this."

Jimmy Watkin was a smooth-talking ex-actor who could charm a rattlesnake out of its rattles—that is, if any rattlesnake was ever so unfortunate as to get that close to him. He was a handsome man of twenty-five who had spent several years on the stage in a St. Louis riverfront playhouse. But the pay was never very good, and Watkin soon discovered that an actor's life was not for him.

Through some fortuitous turn of events—fortuitous as far as he was concerned—he had discovered that much more money could be made by raiding the thriving Missouri River trade and hauling the stolen cargo into Indian country where watered-down whiskey, worn-out rifles, and cheap foofaraws could be traded for valuable beaver pelts, bearskins, and buffalo hides.

Watkin's smile spread out like oil on water.

The scowling faces around him showed that these Indians wanted nothing more than to have an excuse to run the white traders through and then commandeer the trade goods that filled the keelboats drawn up along the muddy riverbank. More than once Jimmy Watkin's smooth tongue had talked their fat out of the fire, and reluctantly Smitter backed off.

"Seems to me we have a bit of a misunderstanding here, Chief Eagle-head," Watkin began, addressing the older headman of the party that had come down to the river to meet the traders. "I thought we agreed on a price of one hundred pelts for a keg of whiskey. That's a fair price. Ask any man along the river."

But the chief was obviously not impressed by other men's opinions. "And rifles," Eagle-head reminded him, scowling.

"Yes, of course. The rifles too. You and your men have brought in two hundred and thirty-seven pelts. We have given you two kegs of top-notch Kentucky whiskey, and five fine St. Louis rifles, just like we agreed on."

Eagle-head shook his head. "No. We bring more beaver skin. You give us more whiskey."

Smitter said to Watkin, "He expects another keg

for them extra thirty-seven pelts. What kind of fools does he take us for?"

"Shut up," Watkin hissed beneath his breath, at the same time keeping an accommodating smile beaming at the Blackfoot warriors, whose hands bristled with weapons. Watkin noted that his own men had taken up rifles and had eased themselves into protected positions behind the cabins of the two keelboats. If push came to shove, Watkin was certain they could outgun these savages, even though the Indians outnumbered them two to one. But killing off your regular customers was no way to run a business.

"You drive a hard bargain, Eagle-head," Watkin moaned, contorting his face woefully in the finest tragedian fashion. "What will we have left to trade to your brothers farther up the river if we give you another keg?"

"Eagle-head not care. Want three whiskey." His demand left no room for dickering.

Watkin frowned. "Let me talk it over with my partner." He and Smitter stepped off a few feet and put their heads together.

"You ain't gonna give that red sonuvabitch what he wants, are you?" Smitter growled.

Watkin gave a short laugh. "I'd like to give him what he deserves. But I got a better idea." When he laid his plan out for Smitter, the other man frowned and reluctantly nodded his head.

"Think you can get away with it?"

"Long enough for us to be miles upriver by time anyone finds out—*if* anyone finds out," Watkin said confidently.

"It's all right by me, I guess."

Watkin glanced at the chief. "All right, Eagle-head. You win. We'll throw in another keg of whiskey."

The chief still didn't crack a smile but merely nodded his head. Watkin called a fellow over named Israel Copp. He gave him instruction in a low voice so that the Indians wouldn't overhear them. Copp hurried to one of the keelboats for the promised payment. Ten minutes later, Copp tramped down the ramp with the keg upon his shoulder and set it next to the first two.

"There it be, Chief," Watkin said, propping a boot atop it. "We got us a deal?"

"Deal, Watkin," Eagle-head declared.

"You drive a hard bargain, Eagle-head." Watkin signaled his men to start loading the skins aboard the boats. "Hurry it up, boys," he prodded. "Got to make another ten miles before the sun sets." The Blackfeet collected the rifles, kegs, and the cartons of cheap trade goods. Watkin called the chief back as the Indians were about to leave.

"Is your wife hereabout, Chief?" he inquired, looking over the faces of the women and children who during the negotiations had remained some distance off but now were gawking at the glass beads and colorful ribbons the men had just acquired.

Eagle-head inclined his head toward a hefty squaw standing nearby.

"Ah! What a lovely creature," Watkin gushed. "Here is something special just for her." From inside his shirt he pulled out a tin hand mirror, then, bowing deeply, he handed it to the Indian woman. "Such beauty demands a looking glass. A gift to you, my dear lady."

She accepted it cautiously, uncertain of the

meaning of his words, but when she glanced into the glass at her gap-toothed image, her wide smile told him she was tickled pink.

"Now we must be on our way," Watkin said, returning to the chief. As the last of the skins were loaded aboard, Watkin leaped to the deck and ordered the men to the poles. The two boats shoved out into the water.

"Put your backs to it, men!" Watkin shouted. The crafts moved sluggishly as the men manning the long poles shoved the keelboats toward the middle of the river. In a few minutes the band of Blackfeet were but a distant speck on the vast shore against an even vaster landscape of endless grass. As the crew pushed the keelboats up against the current, Watkin let out a long, relieved breath. The slap of water against the prow, the grind of the long poles sliding along the gunwales, propelling the sturdy crafts forward, this was the sound of freedom in Watkin's ears. He stepped to the prow and put a foot on the small cannon mounted there, watching the wide waters stretching all around him, broken here and there by the dangerous sandbars that could reach up unexpectedly and grab a boat in its mighty fists. Off to the larboard side an uprooted tree drifted by—a sawyer, as they were known by rivermen.

Watkin went to the top of the cabin where the steersman leaned against the long rudder shaft. "I'll take over from here," Watkin said.

"That was a close one, Cap," Israel Copp said, coming up alongside the taller man.

"Close?" Watkin threw back his head and laughed. His yellow hair glinted in the sunlight and his bright blue eyes flashed like deep mountain lakes. "Those simple savages are no more than children. Taking their furs for a few rusty rifles and some watered-down whiskey is about the next-best thing to stealing."

Copp looked concerned. "Maybe, Cap. But what's going to happen when they discover that third keg holds only river water?"

"We'll be long gone by then, Israel. And anyway, those savages will most likely be too drunk by the first two kegs to care."

"Not hardly, not the way you went and cut that whiskey with good old Missouri River rye."

Watkin grinned. "You worry too much, Copp."

"Maybe, but this here scalp is the only one I got. I'd like to keep it a while longer, if you please."

Watkin laughed again, then he frowned down at the long pole in his hands. "This rudder is about as useless as teats on a boar at this slow pace." He glanced skyward. "And there isn't a blessed breeze anywhere to be found. Tell the men to put in to shore and break out the ropes. Looks like we'll have to cordelle these boats a ways, mate."

They angled for a copse of cottonwood trees and broke out the long ropes. With one end of the rope attached to the tall mast, six stout fellows from each boat took the other ends over their shoulders and started along the shore, pulling the keelboats up the river.

Watkin went down into the cabin and sat at a rough table. The room had four windows on either side with heavy burlap curtains drawn over them. After lighting a lamp, Watkin pulled out a ledger book and wrote in it: *Two hundred and thirty-seven beaver pelts from Chief Eagle-head's band for five rifles, two kegs of whiskey . . . and one keg of river water,* he added as a humorous aside.

Watkin grinned. Life was good. He was well on his way to becoming a rich man, and no one was going to stop him now. He glanced contentedly around the cabin at the trade goods still left to peddle to the ignorant savages along this river, then shut the ledger and went topside to check on the progress of his boat, the *River Maid,* and Smitter's craft, the *Warrior,* following along a few hundred yards downriver.

"You'd think that after all we've been through this winter, Kit, you'd want to stay settled down in one place for a while longer," Gray Feather groused as his stout gray pony carried him away from the mountains of his mother's ancestral home, toward the land where he had spent much of his young adult life, the world of the white man—his father's world. "At least while we were camped with Bridger and the others, there was safety in numbers."

"I don't take to standing at a hitching rail very long, Gray Feather. You know that."

"Maybe so, but this here is Blackfoot country, in case you haven't been paying attention. And Blackfeet scalp white men—and Utes too, if they can lay a hand on them."

Riding a tall dun, Kit Carson glanced over and gave his friend a quick grin, recalling the first time he'd laid eyes on Gray Feather. It had been more than two years past now, but even so, Kit had a perfect vision of an Indian dressed in a frock coat, holding his tall, black hat to his head with one hand while the other clutched the reins of a pounding horse streaking across the Laramie

Plains, half a tail's length ahead of a Cheyenne war party. "Seems to me I recollect you do a fair job of outrunning angry Injuns."

"You're talking about those Cheyenne, aren't you? Well, if it wasn't for you and Mr. Jackson showing up when you did, this scalp of mine would be decorating old Yellow Wolf's lodge pole right now."

Kit grimaced at that. His partner then had been a huge man named Bull Jackson. Bull had died fighting those Cheyenne. Thinking back on it now, Kit was struck by the similarities between Bull and Gray Feather. Both had a mighty strong hankering for reading and a flair for words long enough to gag a buffalo. In spite of that, Kit had grown close to both men, even though he himself could hardly read three words strung together. Kit put the incident out of his mind, burying it deep in his memory, and changed subjects. "You know I promised Charlie Bent last spring that I'd ride up north when I got a chance and take a gander at the trading posts up thar for him."

"Yes, I know. He's building himself a trading house down on the Arkansas River and he wants to learn more about the competition out west." Gray Feather let out a long laugh. "As if there isn't enough commerce in this huge country to keep everyone happy. Fort Lewis is a thousand miles away from Bent's new trading house, for pete's sake."

Kit only smiled. "I can't say as I understand the mind of a man of Charlie's nature . . . what did you call it the other day?"

"Entrepreneurial?"

"Entrepreneurial. Yep, that's it." Kit tried the

word out a few times, but he never could get it to flow off his tongue with such liquid ease as Gray Feather had just done. "All I know is that Charlie asked for my help and I intend to give it."

Gray Feather looked out across the vast grassland they were crossing. There was not a tree in sight, only endless, rolling prairie. "I can understand that. You're a man of your word, Kit, and that's one of the things I admire about you. I only see one problem in your plan."

"Oh? What's that?"

"Fort Lewis is clear up north of here at the headwaters of the Missouri River, more than a hundred miles above Fort Union. So why are we riding *east*?"

"You said it yourself. Both Fort Union and Fort Lewis are on the Missouri. I just figured we'd trot on over to that big river and take a look at it. I've never seen the Missouri this far above its mouth, and I hear tell in places it's still nearly half a mile wide."

"Half a mile wide and all of about knee-deep to a yearling colt," Gray Feather added sarcastically.

"Afterwards we can follow it north to where we're going."

Gray Feather shook his head. "You'll ride a hundred miles out of your way just to take a look at a wide, muddy river? Sometimes I don't know why I tag along with you."

"Because you're a loyal friend, Gray Feather, and that's one of the things I admire about *you*."

"But this is Blackfoot country! And here we are traipsing across it without even a sliver of cover anywhere in sight. We'd have been safely to Fort Union by now if we had just stuck to the Powder River and rode north. We're going to get ourselves killed, Kit."

"It's been almost a week since we left Bridger and the others back on the Powder, and so far we haven't seen hide nor hair of Bug's Boys."

"Maybe, but they're out here, and you know it."

A Blackfoot hunting party *could* show up at any moment, and he and Gray Feather *were* taking a chance crossing this country alone, just the two of them out here. Kit knew it, but during the winter he'd had a flare-up of a mighty bad case of wanderlust. It was a disease that had infected him early on in life, and when it struck, there was only one cure. Wanderlust was an inherited affliction, plaguing the entire Carson clan, always driving them westward. West from Scotland to Ireland. West again from Ireland to America. West still later from Pennsylvania to Kentucky by way of North Carolina, then west finally to Missouri. And here Kit was, three generations later and yet another thousand miles farther along on that journey, always chasing after the setting sun.

"This is a big country, Gray Feather. Lots of space for men to move around in without running into each other. And that's the way I like it." Kit looked around at the wide sea of grass, greening up now after a cold winter just past. The ground was still damp from snow melt and a thunderstorm that had passed by a day before. As he made a sweeping scan he spied a herd of buffalo far off to the west, and another herd of grazing antelope about a mile to the south. But not a single Blackfoot.

"Say, what's that, Kit?"

Kit had been studying the antelope, thinking

that some fresh meat might be nice right about now. They'd been living off of dried elk meat for so long that he'd almost forgotten what the tenderloin of a young antelope roasted over a low flame tasted like. Gray Feather's question, and the sudden note of urgency in it, brought Kit's head around.

"What?"

Gray Feather pointed to the east. Kit pulled down the brim of his hat to shade his eyes and studied the smudge of black rising up from behind a distant ridge.

"Looks like smoke," Gray Feather said.

"Looks like a lot of smoke. Like thar's a big campfire burning out yonder."

"Campfire? Blackfeet?"

Kit didn't answer as he studied the smoke climbing into the clear, blue sky. There was something vaguely familiar in that column of smoke, but searching his brain, Kit could not for the life of him recall what it was.

"I don't know. I reckon it's something we need to get a closer look at."

"We might be riding right into a Blackfoot war party," Gray Feather warned with not just a little alarm in his voice.

"That's a fact," Kit answered, urging his horse on, angling slightly to the north toward the rising land that hid the source of the smoke.

Distances on the open prairies can be deceiving. The ridge that appeared only a mile or so away turned out to be much farther. As the landscape dipped and climbed, the smoke disappeared then reappeared. After a few miles, grass gave way to a scattering of cottonwood trees that thickened into a forest. Kit suspected they were nearing a river. The air held the smell of water. He and Gray Feather slowed their animals to a walk and rode on cautiously. At any second Kit expected to come upon the source of the smoke.

Suddenly he reined to a stop. For a long moment both men sat astride their horses, straining to identify the strange sound that they heard coming from not far ahead.

Tapping his horse's flanks, Kit moved carefully ahead. The cottonwoods parted and one last grassy ridge separated the two trappers from a river that Kit had caught a glimpse of earlier. It was the Missouri River. He was sure of it. The smoke was pumping skyward from just beyond the rise. Kit and Gray Feather swung to the ground and sprinted the last few hundred feet up the rise, keeping low to the ground as the crest of it appeared just ahead.

They crossed the last few feet on their hands and knees. "Well, thar's your Blackfeet," Kit said, pointing down at the river and grinning.

Gray Feather grinned too. "Will you look at that."

"It's called tech-nol-ogy," Kit said, picking one of the longest words he knew for Gray Feather's sake.

"It was called *Pelenore* by the Chickasaw."

"Pelenore? What does it mean?"

"Literally translated, it means 'Fire Canoe'."

"Whal, I can see how they might call it that," he said, looking down at the puffing boat sitting upon the broad river below. The steamer was a long, wide, side-wheeler with towering twin smokestacks coughing black smoke into the blue sky.

Behind the stacks were a pair of shorter stacks venting gray puffs of steam. She had two decks, one on top of the other, with a pilothouse perched atop the uppermost deck. The boat was painted white all over except for a word scrawled in red across her paddle box. The boat's main deck was laden with crates and barrels, some of them covered by canvas tarpaulins. At the moment the boat seemed to be straining with all the power its steam engines could give, stirring up a muddy wake that already stretched far down the river. In spite of her effort, she had not moved even one foot.

"Appears to be having some trouble," Kit noted as he watched the paddles beating the water into a muddy froth. But the boat still wouldn't budge. The harder the paddles chopped, the blacker the smoke that poured out of the boat's twin stacks. All along her deck were men shoving long poles into the water, straining at them as if trying to push the boat back off of a hidden sandbar.

"It's run aground," Gray Feather surmised.

"Can you read that word across her paddle box?" Kit asked. "That would be her name."

"*Zenith*. She's called the *Zenith*."

"Reckon we ought to go down and see if we can't lend a hand, don't you?"

"I think so. I'd like to have a closer look at that boat," Gray Feather said enthusiasticly.

They returned to their horses, and as they climbed back into their saddles, Kit said, "I thought that smoke looked familiar." He shook his head, amazed that he hadn't recognized it at once. "I've seen it plenty of times on the lower Missouri, but I never expected to find a riverboat this far north. A few have tried it, but only a couple have made it so far. As I recollect, the steamer *Yellowstone* was the first to make Fort Union a year or so ago."

"How do you know that?"

"The *Yellowstone* is owned by the American Fur Company. I heard tell of it at the rendezvous last summer," Kit said as they rode down the long slope to the bank of the wide Missouri River, where a dozen or so folks who had been put ashore stood waiting, watching the mighty struggle between machine and nature being played out before them.

Chapter Two

The sound of escaping steam and thrashing paddles made Kit think of an old-time battle between a fire-breathing dragon and a knight in shining armor, just like in the stories his mother used to read to him from the big book of fairy tales she kept on the mantel right next to the family Bible. So enthralled were the watchers on shore that they did not hear Kit and Gray Feather ride up until the two mountain men were practically in their midst. Then one of the passengers, a pretty, young woman of perhaps eighteen, turned at the sound of their horses. She was holding an armful of freshly plucked wildflowers, and at the sight of them she let out a startled gasp.

And at that everyone turned.

Kit reined up and settled his long buffalo rifle across the saddle. "Good morning, ma'am," he said to the lady, who for the moment was quite speechless. His worn and grease-stained buckskins and weathered beaver felt hat must have been an unexpected sight to these people. He'd been all winter in the mountains, and almost three years since spending any time at all in civilization. But it was Gray Feather who was receiving the close scrutiny.

Two of the men were armed. They hitched their rifles into their hands and came over.

"Hello, mister," one of them said cautiously. "Didn't expect to see a white man out here." He spoke to Kit, but his gaze was slanted toward Gray Feather.

Kit gave a short laugh. "Whal, that makes two of us. We thought you might be a Blackfoot war party." His friendly reply helped break the tension. The small crowd chuckled, and the men with the rifles relaxed a bit.

"My name is Warren Randle. I'm a clerk with the American Fur Company." Randle was a short, stocky man with thick black hair and a bull neck. He wore a green and black plaid vest whose buttons strained at his belly. "We're bound for Fort Union with a load of trade goods—that is, if Captain Stromberg ever manages to get his boat off of that sandbar." The man extended a hand.

Kit took it in friendship. "My name is Christopher Carson, but folks just generally call me Kit. We're recently off the Powder River where we wintered over. Gray Feather and me are heading for Fort Union as well."

"Gray Feather?" Randle's view shifted. "I figured him for an Injun."

"Injun?" Gray Feather wagged his head. "Why is it that so many white men insist in dropping double vowels and replacing them with a single 'u'?"

They stared, momentarily lost for words. The second man holding a rifle found his tongue first. Looking back at Kit, he said, "You have gone a mite out of your way, haven't you?" He was taller and thinner than the clerk, and wore a plain brown sack coat and brown trousers. Judging by his hands and weathered face, Kit figured him to be a man who worked out of doors a lot.

"I don't believe I caught your name."

"It's Williams. Marcus Williams."

Kit explained his reason for his detour. When he mentioned Jim Bridger's name, a third man pushed his way ahead of the bright-eyed, attentive young lady, taking her gently by the shoulder as he moved past. He was medium-built, wearing a funny, checkered cap with a wide, round top and an odd little flap at its center, a tan canvas frock, and a red scarf tied around his neck.

"Did I hear you say that you wintered with Jim Bridger?"

Kit shifted his attention to the man. There was an eagerness in his wide blue eyes—eyes about the same shade of blue as the woman's. Curiously, his jacket seemed splattered with various colors.

"That's right."

"Mr. Carson, do you know Jim Bridger well?"

"Gabe and me have ridden together some, trapped beaver together, fought Injuns together a few times. I reckon I know him as well as any man out here."

"That's wonderful!" In his enthusiasm he remembered his manners. "I'm sorry, my name is Jerome Heath, and this is my daughter, Charlotte."

"Pleasure to meet you, and you, ma'am," Kit added with extra feeling, doffing his hat to the comely lady. He was struck by her auburn hair, which had been tied up with a blue ribbon. For so many years now he'd known only the *senoritas* of New Mexico or Indian women of the plains and mountains, both of whom had hair the color of a raven's wing. Kit had nothing against black hair, but her reddish-brown locks were a very pleasant alternative now, and he stared at her a mite longer than he should have.

She smiled prettily in return.

The fourth man there spoke up, breaking the spell that Charlotte Heath had momentarily cast over him. "Best be careful, Mr. Carson, or Mr. Heath there will have you posing like a statue."

Again the small group chuckled.

Jerome Heath said, "I'd like to talk to you further about Mr. Bridger, if you wouldn't mind."

Kit couldn't figure out this fellow's fancy for Bridger, but he agreed to continue the conversation. Looking over at the struggling riverboat, he said, "Got yourself hung up on a bar, I see."

Randle snorted in derision. "Seems that old Captain Stromberg has a habit of running his boat up onto a bar every few miles. I'm already a week behind getting the company's supplies up to Fort Union, and the river is falling fast. When we get home I'm going to advise Mr. Chouteau not to lease the *Zenith* in the future."

"He can't help it. It's this ever-changing river. At least the captain has the good sense to put all of us ashore when he attempts to free the boat," Charlotte said in the captain's behalf. "We all know the dangers," she finished ominously, as if everyone there understood what she meant.

"Perhaps we can be of some help," Gray Feather offered. "We've two strong horses. If you have enough rope aboard we can hitch our animals to the stern of the *Zenith* and help pull her free."

"He sure don't talk like an Inju—er, Indian," Williams commented.

"No," Randle agreed, "but he does have a wonderful idea. And it just might work. I'll row out and tell Captain Stromberg." Randle climbed into a skiff that had been pulled up onto the riverbank. Williams and the fourth man, whose name Kit had not yet learned, pushed it out into the flow. Rowing hard, Randle made his way across the current to the marooned riverboat. A man aboard the *Zenith* tossed out a line and hauled the little skiff into the boat's fenders. Two minutes later, Randle and a big, gray-bearded fellow stepped back into the skiff and Randle ferried him to shore.

Captain Stromberg was a large man of perhaps sixty years with a solid, honest handshake. He face was engulfed in a huge white beard reminiscent of the paintings Kit had seen of Father Christmas. He wore dark trousers, a sweat-stained white cotton shirt unbuttoned down to the middle of his chest, and an equally sweat-stained blue hat with a short, stiff bill.

"Rocky Mountain boys, are you?" Stromberg boomed in a deep, friendly voice.

"We're fresh out of winter quarters and stretching our legs some. My name is Kit Carson, and this is my friend, Gray Feather. We seen your smoke some miles back and came on over to have a look."

Stromberg frowned. "It's this damned river!" he growled, then he grimaced and glanced at Charlotte. "Pardon my language, ma'am."

But it didn't appear that Charlotte Heath had even noticed the captain's oath. Her attention since his arrival had been centered on Kit.

"You run her one season and make charts and you think you know what she looks like, but when you come back the next season, the fickle lady has changed completely. What scant charts I have of her are practically worthless six weeks after they're plotted. I understand you've offered to lend a hand and your animals to help free the *Zenith*," Stromberg said.

"It's a mighty big boat you have thar, Captain Stromberg, and I don't know how much help we'll be, but if you think it will work, Gray Feather and me are willing to give it a try."

"We have been able to rock her and push her back a few yards already. Your horses just might be enough to nudge her off of that bar."

In short order Stromberg brought a line ashore, and using folded blankets to protect the horses, Kit and Gray Feather contrived makeshift harnesses and hitched the animals to the ropes. Now that there was a connection between the *Zenith*'s stern and the shore, the passengers lent a hand as well, grabbing the rope along its length. At a signal the steamer belched a massive cloud of smoke into the air while at its open furnaces men began heaving wood into the fires.

The big paddle-wheels began to revolve in reverse, slowly at first, then rapidly picking up speed. Gray Feather took charge of the horses, urging them on as the men and one woman added their muscle to the task. Kit anchored the heel of his moccasin into the twisted root of a cottonwood tree and strained against the thick rope, muscles bulging beneath his buckskins, teeth gritting, eyes squinting nearly shut. His face reddened as cords of muscle stood out against his neck.

"Yah . . . yah!" Gray Feather shouted, then reverted to some Ute words directed at his pony. The stout little horse seemed to understand what was required of him. Slowly, Kit felt the line move. A few inches at first, then a foot, and another . . . and another . . .

"We're doing it!" Randle cried out.

The small movement spurred them on to greater effort. The boat slid backward another two feet, then with a jolt the rope went suddenly slack and the *Zenith* was backing off the sandbar under her own power. A cheer arose from the people onshore, echoed back at them from the crew aboard the boat.

Kit stretched his muscles and arched his back. Out on the river the steamer moved into deeper water, made a graceful pirouette in the middle of the river, then reversed engines and steamed slowly toward shore: Its prow gently nudged into the muddy shore not ten feet from bank, and at once two crewmen wrestled a loading ramp into place and lowered it to the bank.

Captain Stromberg marched down it, grinning. "We done it. You boys and your horses made the difference. I'm most grateful you two showed up when you did."

As Stromberg was thanking Kit, Gray Feather was eyeing the ramp with bald-faced curiosity, like a wide-eyed boy with his nose pressed against a candy store's window glass.

"It wasn't only Gray Feather and me. Everyone here had a hand in it," Kit answered, looking at the faces around him. Everyone appeared eager to be on their way.

Randle said, "Mr. Carson and his friend are headed up to Fort Union too, Captain. Considering their help, maybe you'd want to give them a ride."

The offer brought immediate joy to Gray Feather's face. He was obviously itching to explore this fascinating mechanical marvel and learn all about its workings. Kit was curious too, but he had heard something else in Randle's generous proposal. Randle was in charge of getting the company's supplies up to Fort Union, and with the *Zenith*'s apparent propensity for sandbars, having a couple of extra strong backs, and even stronger animals, along could do nothing but help him accomplish his goal.

Just the same, Kit was open to the notion, as he'd never ridden on a riverboat before.

"I think that's a bully idea," Stromberg declared. "How about it, gentlemen, would you care to ride the rest of the way in comfort and ease upon my boat?"

"Of course they would." This came from Charlotte Heath, who had spoken before she had thought of how bold it would sound. She glanced down at once, clutching her armful of wildflowers against her bosom.

Kit grinned at seeing a bit of color come to

Charlotte's cheeks. "Whal, that's right generous of you, Captain." He didn't have to ask Gray Feather what he thought of the offer, for it was obvious he was going to have to pry the curious Indian off the boat if he refused Stromberg's invitation. "Reckon we will ride along with you."

"Fine, fine! Now, everyone get back aboard while my men bring on more fuel wood. We've room enough on deck for your horses, gentlemen, although when we stop for fuel you might want to take them to grass."

Gray Feather didn't have to be invited twice. Barely remembering to grab up his rifle, he scrambled up the gangplank, leaving Kit behind to unhitch the horses and take them aboard by himself.

It was a strange sensation, and it took some getting used to, sort of like sliding along on ice—or at least that was as close to describing it as Kit was able to come. He'd never before experienced traveling in such a smooth manner. Never on horseback, and certainly never while riding in a coach or upon a heavily sprung wagon. No, this was something entirely new to him, and he relished the feeling. And the power! The twin steam engines throbbed mightily through the deck and up through the soles of his moccasins where he stood against the larboard railing, watching the bleak shoreline passing swiftly by.

The speed was something else that was new to him. The *Zenith* must have been traveling at a full eight miles per hour!

Amazing, he thought.

All about him swirled mechanical sounds and mechanical lurches and mechanical smells, and while it filled his senses with a whole new world with which he'd previously had very little contact, a part of him wasn't so sure he liked it. He could see that very soon he would be relishing the wide, quiet wilderness where the sounds of man-made contraptions could not invade.

"You look like a man with a problem, Mr. Carson," Captain Stromberg said, coming up behind Kit. Stromberg stopped by the railing alongside him and took in a deep, exhilarating breath and let it out all at once. "The river! The smell and the feel of it gets into a man's blood, it does!"

"I was just thinking how all this clinking and clanking and puffing might get under a man's skin after a while, like a bur in a saddle blanket."

"Oh, it gets under a man's skin, all right," Stromberg admitted, chuckling, "but not like a burr at all. Almost like a . . ." He had to pause to think, then, with a glint in his eyes, he said, "Almost like a beautiful woman." Stromberg ran a hand along the painted railing and patted it affectionately.

Kit laughed. "Whal, I don't have to worry about that happening to me."

"Are you not enjoying the trip?"

"Oh, it's not that at all. It's a long sight easier than straddling a horse ten hours a day, and I don't have to keep an eye peeled in every direction for them Blackfeet, neither. And I reckon sleeping on that bunk you offered to us will be more comfortable than the cold hard ground. It's just that I'm not sure I could ever tolerate all the noise for very long."

"Noise?" Stromberg had a genuinely perplexed look on his face. "What noise?"

"Mean you don't hear it?"

He gave Kit a blank look.

"It's those thumping steam engines, and those grinding paddle wheels, and the rush of steam from those black stacks away up thar."

Stromberg tilted his head back and looked up at the steam vents, sending forth their gray puffs in a syncopated rhythm with the pounding engines. "I reckon that after a while a man stops hearing all of those noises," he said finally. "I don't hear them, at least not consciously. It's only when they change somehow that I hear them. Then I have to find out why they have changed, and fix the problem. After a while you can tell when everything is working smoothly by the simple fact that you *don't* hear the sounds anymore, Mr. Carson. But there is one sound that I am always on the alert for."

"What might that be?"

Stromberg hooked a thumb over his shoulders at the nearby furnaces where crewmen were busily tossing wood through the open maw of their iron doors. "It's those boilers that I listen for," he said. "So long as they stay quiet, I'm happy. But once they begin to creak and groan, that's when the hairs at the back of my neck straighten up. When you hear them start to shriek like a banshee, that's the time to abandon ship without looking back."

Stromberg's sudden soberness made Kit's skin crawl. "Why is that, Captain?"

"It means the boilers are about ready to blow. I've heard that sound only once in my life, and I was one of the lucky ones. I jumped overboard a moment before the whole thing blew sky-high. But even so, I didn't escape scot-free." He pulled up one leg of his trousers and showed Kit the ugly scar that covered his entire calf with shriveled, pink skin. "The steam caught me as I was diving under the water. This is what it did to me in only a brief half second. But like I said, I was one of the lucky ones."

Kit glanced worriedly from the mangled flesh to the black boilers not more than two dozen feet away.

Stromberg laughed. "Now you *really* look like a man with a problem, Mr. Carson."

He gave a wry grin. "I suddenly feel like I'm riding atop a powder keg."

"Well, it's not quite that bad. And it rarely happens while the boat is moving under power. It has, but not as a rule, you understand. No, the time to worry about it is when a boat is first shoving off."

"Why's that?"

"Opening the throttle pumps cold water into the boilers. It's the sudden rise in pressure from that water turning to vapor that can cause a boiler whose volume has been reduced by mud to burst, Mr. Carson. Steam power is not something to be trifled with." Stromberg laughed. "But it's not something to worry yourself about, either. I've not lost a boat yet—to a boiler explosion, that is."

Kit returned his gaze to the passing riverbank and wondered if he wouldn't rather have taken his chances with the Blackfeet than aboard this floating powder keg. Then an odd-shaped hill drew his attention. He looked at it once, then a second time. "That's strange."

"What is?" Stromberg inquired.

"Whal, I could have sworn that we passed by

that very same hill nearly an hour ago. But that can't be possible . . . can it?"

"Possible? Not only is it possible, but in fact you are absolutely correct. We did pass that point an hour ago."

Kit looked bewildered.

Stromberg grinned and said, "Come on up to the pilothouse and I'll show you how it can happen."

Chapter Three

"The Missouri River is one of the twistingest and most contrary streams ever made, Mr. Carson," Stromberg said as he opened the covers of a huge, leather-bound chart book that sat upon a ledge in the pilothouse. He flipped through the pages. Each one contained a small section of the river, drawn by hand, with various points labeled, and notations made in the margins concerning water depth, the location of sandbars, and prominent features along the way.

From the *Zenith*'s pilothouse Kit had a wide, unobstructed view of the river all around him. Two other men were there with them. Gunderson Moore was a tall, gaunt-faced man whom Stromberg had introduced as the boat's pilot. The younger gent, not much older than nineteen, was named Joseph LaBarge. LaBarge was presently manning the helm; a huge wheel that disappeared partway into a long cutout in the floor. He worked for Pratte, Chouteau and Company, and in spite of his young age LaBarge had already spent a year trapping for Pratte and Chouteau's American Fur Company, and was now, according to Stromberg, an apprentice steersman. Moore just called him his "cub pilot."

"You see, Mr. Carson," Stromberg said, pressing a particular page of the book flat and stabbing it with his thick finger, "this here is that knobby hill you just saw. It's even got a name to us along the river. Broken Skull Reach, we call it. Now look here. See how the river flows?" Stromberg traced the Missouri, which swept in near the hill at one point, then turned back away, making a wide four-mile loop to the east before sharply curving back on itself and practically retracing its steps to Broken Skull Reach.

"I see what you mean, Captain. We traveled more than eight miles out and back and only covered the same distance as a man might cover riding his horse but a quarter of a mile across this narrow piece of ground."

Stromberg grinned and gave a low chuckle. "Like I said, it's the twistingest and most contrary river ever made. That's why it is the longest river in the United States and all of its territories."

"I think Gray Feather and me might make better time on horseback," Kit mused aloud.

"You might at that," agreed Stromberg.

That gave Kit something to mull over. But before he'd had time to ponder the matter, there came a knock on the pilothouse door.

"Come on in," Stromberg bellowed as he closed the big book. Jerome Heath and his daughter stepped inside, filling the tiny room nearly to overflowing.

"Yes, Mr. Heath? You wish to see me?"

"Er, well, Captain Stromberg, it is actually Mr. Carson I wish to speak with. I saw the two of you come up here. I hope I'm not interrupting anything."

Kit was feeling claustrophobic in the cramped pilothouse and he welcomed an excuse to remove himself from it. "The captain and me are just finished," he said. "We can talk outside." He led the other two onto the flat roof, which served as a second-story deck of sorts. There was a big bronze bell mounted forward of the pilothouse, a couple of low chimneys from stoves below, and a confusion of hooks, eyebolts, hog chains, and steel cables, all of which served in some way to anchor the tall smokestacks in place. Aft, a staircase descended to the deck below.

Even way up there, Kit could feel the steady *thump, thump, thump* of the engines two decks below. It occurred to him just then that he had not seen Gray Feather since they boarded the riverboat.

"Mr. Carson," Heath began at once, his enthusiasm boiling over like a kettle of porridge left too long on the stove. "I wonder if I might bother you for a moment."

"I've got all day, Mr. Heath, and it don't look like I'm going anywhere except sideways on this crazy river. Speak your mind."

"I'm an artist. I've come all the way from Pennsylvania to capture on canvas this river and the colorful people who inhabit this land. That includes Indians, the rivermen like Captain Stromberg, and, of course, the trappers like yourself."

"Didn't some fellow named Catlin come through here a year or so ago doing that?"

"Why, yes. George Catlin. We've met once or twice. But there is so much to show the people back east that one artist could never do a complete job of it. There is great interest in what is happening out here in the Purchase. We've heard a little about the exploits of fellows like Colter and Bridger."

"So that's why you wanted to talk to me about old Gabe."

"Gabe? Is that what he is called by his trapping companions?"

Kit gave a short laugh. "He's called by many names, but Gabe is the only one I dare use in polite company." He smiled and slanted an eye at Charlotte, who freely smiled in return.

"Mr. Bridger is rather famous back east," Heath went on.

Charlotte said, "Perhaps someday Mr. Carson will be famous too."

Kit grinned at her. "I don't expect that will ever happen, ma'am. I'm just a simple trapper. I'll never be famous like Jim Bridger. Don't know as I'd even want that kind of fame. A good rifle, a good horse, a warm blanket, and a dry roof over my head is all I really need."

"Well, just the same," Jerome went on, "I want to paint your picture, if you wouldn't mind. And to hear a little about what Mr. Bridger—old Gabe, as you call him—is like."

"Like I said, I'm not going anywhere anytime soon."

All at once the big boat slowed. Kit heard the paddle wheels grind to a halt and the constant splashing suddenly cease. The boat seemed to settle heavily in the water, and from somewhere below came a rushing high-pitched whistle as massive amounts of steam vented from the gauge cocks.

"What has happened now?" Charlotte said with a hint of exasperation.

Kit remembered the warning that Stromberg had given him, but although the high-pitched whistling was ominous, it didn't sound anything at all like what he'd imagined a banshee wail sounded like. They moved to the railing and looked down where the rising steam warmed Kit's face.

"Another delay," Heath said glumly.

But Kit figured that it would be Randle, the agent with Pratte, Chouteau and Company, who would be most annoyed by another delay.

As the big boat settled to a stop, men down below hopped to her fenders and began shoving her into shore, using long poles.

"It's not another sandbar?" Kit asked.

"I don't think so," Jerome said. "It didn't feel like we hit anything."

At that moment Captain Stromberg emerged from the pilothouse and started down a ladder to the deck below. Kit, Jerome, and Charlotte followed on his heels.

They caught up with him below in the engine room, where, not surprisingly, Kit also located his long-lost friend.

Gray Feather came over and said, "What an amazing piece of machinery this is, Kit! Mr. Hamner, the chief engineer, has been telling me all about it."

"Uh-huh," Kit replied, watching the captain and Hamner locked in serious conversation.

"Do you know that there is over a hundred pounds of pressure per square inch in those boilers?"

Kit shot him a worried glance. "You didn't hear no banshee wailing, did you?"

That gave Gray Feather pause. "Banshee?"

"What happened to stop the boat?"

"Um, I think there's some problem or another with the boilers," Gray Feather said.

Across the way Stromberg's deep voice rumbled. "All right, Mr. Hamner, we'll put in to shore and get the job done. Better safe than sorry, I always say." He strode out of the engine room past Kit and the others and out onto the main deck, where he ordered a man to take a line ashore.

The boat was in a commotion, but Kit gathered by Stromberg's control of the situation that whatever had gone wrong hadn't really put the *Zenith* in any immediate danger. A crewman jumped into the river, which only came to his waist, and carried a rope ashore. He tied it off on a stout tree growing down by the water's edge. At the bow of the boat two other men shoved long oak poles into slots in the capstan and began walking a circle on the deck, taking up the slack in the line and winching the big boat into shore.

After the excitement subsided and the gangplank had been lowered so that the passengers and crew could go ashore, Kit followed the captain back to the engine room while Gray Feather told him every thing he'd learned so far about steamboats.

"Whal, now that things have settled down, Captain, can you tell us what happened?"

Stromberg glanced up from a big, round, brass gauge that he had been studying closely and managed a quick grin. "Oh, it is nothing to be concerned about, Mr. Carson. We just had a sudden buildup of pressure, that's all. That last bout we fought with that sandbar stirred up so much mud that it got into the boilers. Mr. Hamner had the foresight to open the gauge cocks immediately and vent it off before any damage could be done, but we will have to wait here until the boilers cool down and we can put a man inside there to muck it out."

"Damage? You mean like the boilers blowing up?"

Stromberg laughed. "I see now what's got you concerned. It's that little story I told you earlier. Well, you needn't have worried." He rapped the gauge's glass face with his knuckle. "The pressure was still well below the danger level. See, look here."

Kit peered at the dial Stromberg had been studying a moment before. There was a long needle and a string of numbers that ran from 0 to 250. After the number 125 there was a yellow mark, and at 180 was a red mark.

"The pressure never went over the yellow, Mr. Carson. That's our room for error. It's when the needle creeps up past that red line that we are in real danger."

"Those markings measure the pounds of steam

per square inch of pressure," Gray Feather added. "Mr. Hamner explained it all to me."

"Is two-fifty as high as it can go?" Kit inquired.

"No, no, Mr. Carson. It would never reach two-fifty. The boilers would give way long before that. Probably around two hundred to two-twenty, I should guess, would be the maximum they could withstand."

This line of conversation made Kit uneasy. He preferred to stick to things he understood, like horses. Horses, he reminded himself once again, never blew up under their riders.

On their way down the loading ramp to shore Gray Feather asked Kit what story the captain had been referring to. Kit retold the account of the steamer that had blown up, scalding Stromberg's legs. Gray Feather nodded his head knowingly.

"I've heard of such things happening. I read an account once of a steamer blowing her boilers while leaving the levee at New Orleans. That explosion flung pieces of the boat as far as a quarter of a mile inland."

"A quarter mile?" Kit stepped off the gangplank onto firm ground, grateful for it, and gave a long sigh of relief. "I'm not sure I'm ready for all this new tech-no-logy, Gray Feather. I'm thinking we might just saddle up and ride north. If nothing else, it's bound to cut a hundred miles from the trip, what with the way this river twists and turns and folds back onto itself."

Gray Feather was crestfallen. "You can't really want to leave so soon. Why, there's still so much to learn!"

"That boat is a floating powder keg. I'd sooner

take my chances with wild animals or wild Blackfeet."

Gray Feather tried a different tack. "It's just that you don't understand it, Kit. Once you do, you'll see that it's perfectly safe."

But Kit heard the catch in Gray Feather's voice. "Safe. Why, you don't even believe that yourself."

"Mr. Carson," Jerome Heath called from farther up the shore. "Oh, Mr. Carson." He had set up an easel and a little table, and an opened wooden box displayed bottles of various colors. Now he laid down a brush he'd been holding and hurried over. "Captain Stromberg says we will be tied up here the rest of the day and night. Could I possibly impose on a bit of your time to make a few quick sketches and put some paint to one of my canvases?"

Kit knew that Gray Feather wanted to pursue this debate further, but he for one was ready to get his mind off of riverboats and onto something else.

He allowed Jerome to haul him off by the arm and pose him just so, holding his rifle upright in his right hand with the sweeping bend of the river off to his left. Heath angled his chin toward the river and told Kit to point with his left hand as if he had just spotted something far down the stream. Out of the corner of his eye he saw Gray Feather stroll off with one of the crewmen. He put his friend and the question of whether to stay with the *Zenith* or resume their journey on horseback out of his mind for the time being.

Jerome busied himself making quick bold lines on the canvas with a stub of charcoal. In a few minutes Charlotte showed up, holding some freshly plucked flowers. She looked over her father's shoulder and nodded approvingly.

"You make an excellent subject, Mr. Carson. So dashing!"

Kit nearly blushed. "I see you've taken a fancy to the wildflowers that grow along the river."

"It's a hobby of mine, Mr. Carson. I have brought a plant press along on this trip. I'm collecting all types of plants to bring back with me. Perhaps I will find some new variety that has never been described before."

Kit made a wry smile. Charlotte Heath was sounding a lot like Gray Feather. "That's nice, ma'am."

She stepped to his side and gave him a perky smirk. "You're just being polite. I can see that you don't care anything about flowers."

"Why, that ain't true, ma'am. I think thar right pretty to look at—some of them at least, and mighty useful too. The Indians make all kinds of handy things out of them, from poultices for bullet wounds to healing everything from flux to gout to canker rashes."

"Is that so? I should like to learn more about that."

"It's Gray Feather you should be talking to, then."

"Your Indian friend? He is not anything at all like I expected an Indian to be."

"No, ma'am. He's a strange critter, all right. But he's a right decent fellow."

"He seems well educated."

"It's all that civilized living what done that to him, ma'am. His pa took him back east when he was but a tyke and gave him schoolin'. He went to

Harvard College and come away from thar spouting words big enough to choke a buffler. Just don't mention anything about that English feller, Shakespeare, or Gray Feather's likely to talk your ear off."

"Please try to stand still, Mr. Carson."

"Sorry." Kit stiffened up his pose.

"Tell me more," Charlotte insisted.

"About Gray Feather?"

"No. About yourself."

"Whal, there ain't a whole lot to tell."

"Where are you from?"

"I was born in Kentucky, but I lived most all my life at Boon's Lick in Howard County, Missouri, ma'am. I run away from thar when I was sixteen. Went west to Taos and have remained out west ever since."

"My, how interesting. You must have some wonderful stories to tell."

"I got a few of them. But the one who can really spin a yarn is old Gabe."

"Mr. Bridger? Why do you call him 'Gabe'?"

"It's short for Gabriel, that angel out of the Bible. Jim Bridger is a solemn-faced sort of feller, and us Rocky Mountain boys just figured that Gabriel must be a solemn sort of angel—except, of course, when he goes to tooting that horn of his."

Charlotte laughed, and her sudden smile was bright enough to warm a politician's heart. As Kit reveled in its warmth he happened to glance past her shoulder at the bend in the river beyond. Something moved down there. He squinted hard against the sunlight glinting silvery off the rippling water. Then he saw it again. From around the bend two keelboats came slowly into view.

"Look thar," Kit said, and since he was already in a pointing pose for Heath's picture, her view naturally followed his finger, which happened to be aimed at precisely the place where the keelboats had come into view. "Looks like we're about to have some company."

Slowly the boats came upriver, growing larger as they approached. In a few minutes Kit could make out the men on shore cordelling them along. By this time everyone had been alerted to the new arrivals. Jerome Heath took a break from his work. Kit relaxed out of his stiff stance and strolled, with Charlotte at his side, down to the water's edge where the others were already waiting for the boats.

The keelboats hauled to a stop on the other side of the river and tied off. A few minutes later, a half-dozen men climbed into a small rowboat that had been tethered behind the lead boat and started across the river.

Chapter Four

The first man out of the rowboat was a tall, sandy-haired man with a handsome smile and a confident, erect bearing. He eyed the *Zenith* appreciatively as he came across the beach. Captain Stromberg went out to meet him, and the two men shook hands.

"I'm Jimmy Watkin, captain of the *River Maid*, and this here is my business partner, Captain Rafe Smitter, skipper of the *Warrior*."

"Walter Stromberg. Owner and skipper of the *Zenith*, berthed out of St. Louis. We don't often meet fellow rivermen this far north of Independence. Come on into our camp, gentlemen, and welcome."

"Where you bound, Captain?" Watkin asked. "Fort Union?"

"Yes, that's correct."

"Figured it must be. The only steamers that ever make it this far up the river are those of the American Fur Company." He eyed the big vessel again. "I'll wager you're filled with trade goods for the savages."

"We have some of that, yes. That and supplies to restock the fort's garrison. Powder, lead, rifles, tinware, tobacco, whiskey, flour . . . the usual freight. Enough to carry them through to next spring when the river's running high again and another steamer can push its way up. And you, sir?"

"Me and my partner carry on a little business with the savages. You know, some whiskey, a few old rifles, beads and trinkets for the womenfolk. We take back beaver pelts in trade. It's a small business, not enough to hurt the American Fur Company's business, mind you, but it keeps us going all right."

As Kit watched the three men approach he was aware of Charlotte's keen interest in the newcomers. He was interested in them, too, but probably for a different reason. Every one of the men who had come across on the rowboat carried a rifle, and each had at least one pistol thrust under his belt. They moved past the crew of the *Zenith* and spread out, just like he had seen Comanches do once when they had entered a trappers' camp under a pretense of friendship. That encounter had turned bloody, and Kit had only barely managed to escape with his scalp intact. Over the years Kit had learned to recognize a certain type of man—the kind you ride wide of if you can—and these *hombres* fit that image perfectly.

Charlotte's view had narrowed slightly, and she

had stiffened in some vague, hardly discernible manner. But slight as it was, Kit had noticed it.

"Is there something wrong, Miss Heath?" he asked.

Immediately she shook off her wariness and smiled up at him. "Wrong? Why, whatever could be wrong, Mr. Carson?"

"For a minute thar it looked as if you knew those men."

"I have never seen them before in my life," she assured him. Then, with a pause and a grimace, she added, "But I think I have known men like them. I'm usually a very good judge of character, Mr. Carson, and those two, and the others with them, well, I think they are men whom I would not trust very far. That one, the leader, he's just too smooth to be genuine."

"I'd say you've got him pegged just about right, ma'am." Kit glanced at the lock of his rifle to make sure a cap was still in place. Then he cast about for Gray Feather and spied his partner a few dozen feet away, standing alongside the chief engineer. Kit caught Gray Feather's eye and gave a small nod. The Ute saw Kit's concern, for he made a casual loop around the camp and came up beside Kit.

"What's wrong?"

"Nothing, yet," Kit said softly. "I don't like the looks of these gents, and they're bristling with more firearms than old Colonel Leavenworth had with him when he took his army up again' the Rees in their walled village. Just keep your eyes open and your rifle ready."

By then the three captains had come close enough for Watkin to spy Charlotte standing there. He stopped at once, gazing at her, then strolled over, swept his floppy hat from his head, and bowed deeply from the waist.

"This country holds many surprises, miss," he said, peering openly at the third finger of her left hand, "and I'm always amazed at the beauty I find in the most unlikely places. But today I have discovered the greatest beauty. Your radiance, fair lady, surpasses all. Like a summer's day, only more lovely and more temperate. I am James Watkin, humbly at your service."

Kit rolled his eyes. He'd never heard such fancy words spread out before a lady before. He didn't know what to make of Watkin, except he knew one thing. The man definitely was *not* humble.

"Why, Mr. Watkin. What a nice thing to say," Charlotte gushed.

"Might I be so bold as to ask your name?"

"It is Charlotte. Charlotte Heath."

"Charlotte," he intoned as if savoring the sound of it. "How could I not have realized that such a lovely person as yourself should have a name fit for a goddess atop Mount Olympus? Might I call on you a little while later, Miss Charlotte?"

She smiled. "I'll be here until the boat leaves in the morning, Mr. Watkin."

"Until later." He bowed again, this time more quickly and not so deeply.

When he had returned to the others, Kit gave a long whistle. "That fellow's sure got a golden tongue."

Charlotte was still beaming when she looked at Kit. "He said that my radiance surpassed all. And that it was like a summer's day, only more lovely and more temperate." Still beaming, she added sharply, "That man is so full of bull that I'm afraid I'm going to have to go back to my chambers and clean my shoes."

Her unexpected earthiness startled Kit, and he laughed. "You're the most sensible woman I've met in a long time."

"But they were such flattering words," she admitted.

Gray Feather piped up and said, "Yes, flattering. It's just too bad they weren't his own."

Kit and Charlotte looked at him.

"Actually, the correct quote is, 'Shall I compare thee to a summer's day? Thou art more lovely and more temperate.' " Gray Feather grinned. "Shakespeare."

"You mean to tell me that he stole that line?" she exclaimed.

"Yes, ma'am. Right from Shakespeare's sixteenth sonnet."

"The scoundrel!"

"My guess is you've got that right," Kit agreed wholeheartedly.

Watkin and Smitter were more than just a little curious about the *Zenith,* and like any proud ship's master, Captain Stromberg took them aboard and gave them a tour. He showed off the *Zenith*'s mighty steam engines, and the big boilers where crewmen were busily scraping out the mud that had accumulated. He led them through the long and narrow, but well-appointed, main cabin where the passengers ate their meals. He showed off her sleeping chambers, which, although sparse and tiny by Mississippi River standards, were the height of luxury this far from civilization. But what interested Watkin and Smitter most were the piles of cargo that Stromberg was hauling upriver to the American Fur Company's far-flung trading posts of Fort Union, and then beyond by smaller boats to Fort Lewis.

Afterward, Stromberg invited Watkin, Smitter, and his crew to share dinner with them, for they had plenty of food. The keelboatmen accepted the invitation immediately, and with open friendliness. But just as soon as they were off on their own and huddled together by the rowboat, they let down their genial charade.

"There's enough trade goods aboard that steamer to make us all rich men!" Watkin said, his eyes darting greedily toward the *Zenith*. In the lowering sunlight the riverboat's shadow stretched far out across the swiftly flowing water.

"I counted at least ten cases of rifles," Smitter added.

"Rifles?" Watkin gave a hearty laugh. "Did you see the whiskey? A dozen kegs or more. Enough to keep Eagle-head and every other savage up and down this river drunk for a month!"

"What are we going to do about it?" Copp asked.

"I say we take the boat," Watkin proposed.

"Hmm." Smitter's bushy eyebrows dipped down as he considered this. "That's a bold plan, considering she's carrying a full crew."

"But I didn't see as most of 'em were armed," a fourth man, named Hawk Marcetti, added. He'd gotten the name from his beak of a nose, and from the long, Arkansas Toothpick that he carried under his belt—his claw, as he called it, and a deadly talon it was.

"No, they're not carrying firearms," Watkin

agreed. "But you can bet they'll have them close at hand, what with this being Indian country. Just the same, it's those two borderers who were standing with Charlotte that's got me worried. They don't seem to ever drift very far from their rifles and pistols, and they looked the type who could use them."

"Not to mention their knives and tomahawks, heh?" Smitter added. "But all the rest of them, they'd not put up much of a fight, would be my guess."

"How are we to do it?" another pirate asked, and the men nodded their heads.

"First we need to bring the others across. We'll break out a keg of whiskey—some of the good stuff; our contribution to the meal. We'll eat their food, and when we're all done we'll toast to the captain's good health. After everyone has had a tankard or two and beginning to feel drowsy, some of our boys will slip aboard the *Zenith* and secure her. Then I'll put a pistol to Stromberg's skull and inform everyone that we're taking over."

"What will we do with all of them afterwards?" Hawk asked.

"Can't leave witnesses about, now can we? Careless way to conduct business," Watkin admitted.

The men chuckled.

Watkin continued. "We'll shoot them and feed them to the catfish. Then we'll put fire to the boat. If anyone finds it later, they'll think it was the Blackfeet."

"What about the girl?" Smitter asked. "You were taken with her."

"Ah, yes. The beautiful Charlotte Heath. It would be a shame to pluck such a lovely flower.

We shall take her with us—at least for a little while."

"That can be dangerous, Jimmy," Israel Copp advised. "A word from her would hang us just as surely as that from any of the men."

"Even faster," a shriveled-face pirate with gray whiskers advised. "You know how some folks feel about a woman taken against her will."

Watkin shrugged off the advice. "We won't let her get to any place where her words will matter. We'll get rid of her before that."

"Speak of the devil," Smitter declared, glancing across the small camp. "There she goes now."

Charlotte Heath was strolling casually out of camp, her head tilted toward the ground as if looking for something. In a moment she had wandered up over a small hill and was out of sight. Watkin grinned to the others. "Dangerous country for a lady to be out on her own."

"Then why don't you go and keep the lass company?" Hawk suggested with a smirking leer.

"I just might do that, Hawk. And while I'm off seeing to her needs, you and Copp take the rowboat across and bring one of the keelboats back."

Watkin grabbed up his rifle and wandered casually away, careful to appear to be going in a direction different from Charlotte's—at least until he was out of sight of the camp.

Charlotte was amazed at the variety of flowers she had encountered since leaving the States. Most of them, she was certain, had never been described before, which made this the perfect place for an amateur botanist to come collecting. She had read of the collecting that Lewis and Clark had done on their expedition to explore the Louisiana Purchase, but already she had discovered plants even those two famous explorers had failed to find. Her plant press back in her sleeping chamber aboard the *Zenith* was already bulging. She could hardly wait to get back to Pennsylvania and make a proper catalogue of everything she had collected.

Charlotte stopped and bent down. At the toe of her shoe she had spied a tiny blue flower. It was an aster of some sort, she decided, studying it. But what sort? A perfect specimen for her press! She hummed a lilting tune as she carefully probed the rocky soil with a thin-bladed knife. Slowly she eased the plant from the ground, keeping its roots intact as best she could.

So intent was she on her work that she was not aware that someone had come quietly up behind her . . . until he spoke.

"Indians sometimes kidnap white women."

She spun about, startled, nearly dropping the plant she'd just collected. "Oh, it is you, Captain Watkin," she breathed with a nervous little laugh. "I didn't hear your footsteps."

"And after they have kidnapped them they force the women to live in their tepees, cook their food, clean their lice-ridden skins, bear their children," he continued as if she had not even spoken.

"I sometimes get distracted and lose track of where I am. Have I wandered very far?" Charlotte looked back the way she had come.

"A few hundred yards is all," he said, stepping closer, his eyes focused on hers. "But as you can see, the camp and the boat are no longer in view. No one can see you back behind this ridge. A

Blackfoot war party could have captured you and carried you away without anyone ever knowing it."

Now he was so close that only a scant few inches separated them. He seemed to exude a power that was reaching out to her, an overwhelming force that Charlotte had never experienced before. For a moment all she saw was his broad chest before her. When she looked up, his smile was fixed oddly upon his tight lips. His eyes peered down at her with frightening passion. The lowering sunlight touching his golden hair set it to glowing, as if Watkin were wearing a halo. Charlotte shivered, and suddenly she was terrified of this man. Yet, strangely, she was drawn to him.

"I . . . I think I'd better get back to the boat now," she said, retreating a step.

Watkin closed the distance again. "Why? Now that I'm here you're safe."

She managed an uncertain laugh. "No, I don't think I am safe here with you, Mr. Watkin."

"I frighten you."

This rankled Charlotte, and she squared her shoulders and grabbed back control of her emotions. She had nothing to fear, she reminded herself. Certainly not from this man. She was eighteen years old—almost nineteen—and she could make her own way in life now. She could handle any tall, broad-shouldered, handsome man. . . . Then why did she feel such trepidation?

"Frightened?" She laughed it off lightly. "I'm not frightened of you, Mr. Watkin. I just need to get this plant into my press before it wilts, that's all. But I do appreciate you coming out and reminding me to be more careful and not to wander too far when I go off with my nose to the ground." She laughed again, and inwardly cursed the nervous tremor that slipped out with it. But when she tried to step around him, Watkin cut her off.

"You don't really want to leave just yet?" he said.

Charlotte shivered at his words. Although said as a question, there was something coldly demanding in his low voice.

"I think you'd better let me pass."

"No, you're only pretending that you don't want me. I see the desire in your eyes. You can't fool ol' Jimmy Watkin."

She gasped, shocked by his arrogance. "You may be able to woo some of the ladies with your good looks and smooth way with words, Mr. Watkin, but I see right through your craftiness. Now, let me pass!"

Instead he grabbed Charlotte by the arm and yanked her toward him. As she fought, he twisted her arm up behind her back and smothered her against his chest, his lips pressing hard against hers. She tried to scream, but Watkin muffled her, dragging her to the ground.

Suddenly a strong hand clamped onto Watkin's shoulder and yanked him around. Startled, Watkin swiveled his head about, but it was too late to avoid the fist that was swinging for his chin.

The blow sent the keelboat captain crashing to the ground. Charlotte looked up as Kit Carson stopped at her side with both fists clenched and a scowl pressed deeply into his face.

"I don't know where you were brought up, mister, but back in Missouri we treat women with respect."

Watkin wiped the blood from his split lip and

shot a quick glance to his left where his rifle lay. "Back where I come from a man keeps out of another man's business unless he's prepared to pay the price for nosing in."

"I'll back my action with my fists. Are you ready to do the same?" Kit taunted.

Charlotte scrambled to her feet and out of their way.

Watkin rose to his knees, planting his hands flat on the ground as if preparing to lunge. Instead he grabbed a handful of dirt and flung it into Kit's face, at the same time launching himself at Kit's gut with his head lowered like a rutting Rocky Mountain bighorn's.

Kit scrubbed his eyes as Watkin's weight drove him backward, momentarily knocking the wind out of him. Watkin tumbled to the ground with him, and Kit shot a fist where he calculated the man's chin would be.

He missed. Instinctively, Kit rolled to the left, and the next moment he heard a thump and a howl as the pirate's fist connected with the hard ground instead of Kit's chin. Kit spun around and, still blinded by the dirt, drove both feet in the direction of the howl and connected with his unseen opponent. Watkin let out a loud *oomph*.

Kit backpedaled. Tears had begun to flush his eyes, but he was still groping in the dark. Catlike, he was back on his feet, crouching. He was able to just make out moving shapes against the brighter sky.

Then Watkin loomed directly in front of him. Kit ducked as the man's fist *whoosh*ed overhead. Coming up, Kit found Watkin's belly. It was washboard-hard, but Kit's knuckles made a deep impression in it just the same and sent the fellow stumbling backward. Kit finished scrubbing his eyes, blinking the last of the dirt from them. Quickly he brushed aside the tears that were still flowing freely.

Watkin came barreling back. He was taller than Kit and had greater reach, but Kit was flint-hard and wiry. He'd fought for his life so many times in the past that he hardly noticed that he was outsized. In matters of life and death, size is less of a factor than speed and agility, and Kit had both. They battled back and forth, each holding his own until Watkin suddenly broke off the encounter. At first Kit thought the fellow was giving up. But he was mistaken.

Watkin spun around all at once and dove for the rifle lying nearby. As soon as Kit realized what the man was thinking, he leaped after him.

Watkin swept up the rifle, drawing back the hammer at the same time. Kit reached for the pistol in his belt, only to discover that he'd lost it somewhere in the struggle. Grabbing the tomahawk from his waist, Kit swung out, connecting with the rifle's barrel and knocking it aside just as Watkin's finger was closing on the trigger.

The rifle exploded near Kit's ear with racking pain.

Watkin was quick. He reversed the rifle, grabbed the barrel, hauled back, and took a swipe at Kit's head. If he had connected he'd have split it open like a ripe pumpkin. But Kit was just as quick. His tomahawk rang out against the steel butt plate. The rifle whirled around again, this time catching the short ax by its head and knocking it from Kit's fist.

Kit had only his butcher knife left. He drew it and jumped backward as the rifle swung out. Again and again the long rifle whistled through the air, each time driving Kit back a step. There was no penetrating Watkin's offense short of taking his chances throwing the knife, something he'd rather not attempt except as a last resort.

Then a pistol barked nearby.

Gray Feather was at the crest of the little hill, a smoking caplock in one hand and another in his right, pointing at Watkin.

"Drop the rifle," Gray Feather ordered.

Watkin hesitated, rifle cocked over his left shoulder. Gray Feather drew up and took deliberate aim. "I said drop it, or I drop you."

Watkin slowly put the weapon down. Gray Feather came on as behind him the hill filled with men. Four of them were Watkin's men. But the other ten were from the riverboat. Captain Stromberg strode ahead of them, right behind Gray Feather, glaring fiercely behind his big gray beard.

Kit drew a huge breath and let it out with a great sigh of relief. From behind him Charlotte dashed over to the men, running into her father's arms.

Chapter Five

"Our friendship was given to you freely, and see how you have betrayed it," Stromberg growled, looking a little like Moses must have when he came down from Mount Sinai and discovered the golden calf. They were standing by the river's edge now. Stromberg had ordered their weapons confiscated once he'd learned the cause of the fight. He marched the keelboatmen back aboard the rowboat, which fortunately had not yet left to bring the others across. "All I can say is that it was lucky for you that Mr. Carson showed up when he did. If any harm had come to Miss Charlotte, I swear that I'd have put a rope around your neck and strung you up between the *Zenith*'s stacks."

"You'll pay for this, Stromberg," Watkin snapped, "and you too," he said, spearing Kit with a deadly stare.

Kit said, "You take your boys back where you came from, and we best not see you again."

"You will see me again, Carson. And when you do we will finish this once and for all."

"Enough of this!" Stromberg ordered. "You better go now, Watkin."

"What about our guns?"

"I will leave them for you at Fort Union. If you want them back, you will have to pick them up there."

"How will we defend ourselves until then?"

"I am certain you have enough weapons aboard your keelboats to fend off any hostile attack from Indians. These few rifles and pistols won't make a difference."

With a growl of disgust, Watkin shoved off in the rowboat. As they rowed out into the gloom of the coming night, Stromberg shook his head and said, "We can do without the likes of them on this river."

"This country is full of men like Watkin," Kit observed, thinking back to the few he'd met, recalling a run-in with one in particular, a trapper named Seth Wilson, who had kidnapped a girl from her home in Independence, Missouri, and had taken her out to the Rocky Mountains. Kit had managed to rescue the girl when all others feared her dead. His only regret was that Wilson had escaped, and as far as Kit knew, he was still free somewhere.

They went back to the fires and had dinner. It was the best meal Kit could remember eating in years. The boat's larder was crammed with food impossible to find in the wilderness. More than once during the course of the meal, Jerome Heath profusely thanked Kit for noticing Watkin leaving camp and for having the foresight to follow the scoundrel.

Three or four times during dinner Kit caught Charlotte watching him. She would immediately avert her eyes when he discovered her. It make him nervous and a little uncomfortable—as if his shirt collar were cinched up too tight—except that he wore no collar.

Afterward, she found Kit down by the river staring across the wide, black water at the speck of firelight that marked the keelboatmen's camp.

"Are you worried they will come back?" she asked him.

Kit shook his head. "I don't think Watkin and his men will try anything." The camp had quieted down, and Kit was enjoying the sound of the river whispering peacefully past, accompanied by a chorus of crickets and at least two toads.

"He made his intentions known," she countered.

"He had to make those bold remarks. It's what men like him do to keep their pride when they've been bested."

"I don't know how you can be so calm about it, Mr. Carson. I get gooseflesh just thinking about it."

"Whal, I reckon you're safe enough here with the boat and Captain Stromberg. He and your pa will watch over you like a mamma bear with cubs from here on out. You just need to stop wandering off like you do."

She gave him a wry smile. "I lose my head when

I'm thinking about my collecting. But I will be more careful from now on. I feel safer knowing that you will be nearby, too."

Kit frowned. He'd been thinking it over and had just about decided to quit the boat come morning when it shoved off again. There was no doubting that he and Gray Feather could make much better time on horseback, avoiding all the twists and turns this river was throwing in their path. But there was another matter that he would never care to admit to. He'd become a little skittish over the notion of steam engines, boilers, and the possibility of being blown to kingdom come. His decision to leave the boat was going to disappoint Gray Feather, who was taking in all this new wonderment like a kid let loose in a candy store.

"I've been thinking it over some, Miss Heath, and I reckon that come morning me and Gray Feather will leave the boat." He saw in Caroline's suddenly wide expression that he had disappointed her as well.

"Oh. I'm sorry to hear that," she said evenly, attempting to hide it.

Kit was torn. "It's just that we can make better time cutting straight-arrow north than if we stick to the contrariness of this river."

"I understand."

They stood there peering across the dark river for a long, uncomfortable moment, then Charlotte said, "I think I will turn in now. Good evening, Mr. Carson."

"Evening, ma'am."

Charlotte gathered up her skirts and took the landing stage to the *Zenith*'s main deck, then the stairs up to the promenade that fronted the cabins on the second deck. Kit watched her until she shut the door of her cabin behind her. A few moments later a lamp was turned up and its soft, yellow glow brightened the cotton curtains across her window.

Grimacing at the unpleasant task that lay before him, Kit slung his rifle over his shoulder and strode off to find Gray Feather.

Later that evening, Kit took up Captain Stromberg's offer to use one of the cabins for the night. It had been years since he'd slept in a real bed, and at first he had trouble dozing off. But once he did, he slept like the dead and he didn't wake until the sun was already in the sky.

Kit swung out of bed, amazed that the sun had beaten him. Out on the promenade he paused to look across the river. It was a beautiful sight, with the sun glinting low and silvery across the rushing current. On the far shore he noted with some satisfaction that the keelboats had already shoved off. He looked upriver, but the boats were nowhere to be seen. Watkin and his men must have left some hours earlier.

Coming around the promenade to the shore side, Kit paused to watch the men collecting their belongings and carrying them aboard. Captain Stromberg was speaking with his pilot, Gunderson Moore. Moore's cub pilot, Joseph LaBarge, was there too.

Gray Feather was sitting on a log by the fire, drinking coffee and talking with Hamner, the engineer. Kit frowned when he recalled telling Gray Feather the night before that he wanted to continue their trip on horseback. The Ute had protested, of course, and claimed that although the traveling might be slower, it was certainly safer. Kit let it slip that it might not be safer. Gray Feather had picked up on that right away and wheedled it out of Kit that he was really thinking about saving his hide from a scalding demise, not saving time.

"It's just that you don't understand the principle behind steam power," Gray Feather had countered.

But Kit had stood firm with his decision. Now he had to face his friend—and what would surely be a plea to reconsider. As he started down the gangplank, Kit met Captain Stromberg and the two pilots coming up.

"Mr. Smith tells me you two are not continuing with us," Stromberg said, using Gray Feather's white name. Gray Feather's father had named him Waldo. But his mother had thought Gray Feather a more fitting handle for a boy of Chief Walkara's tribe. The end result was Waldo Gray Feather Smith. In the West he generally went by Gray Feather. He had considered simply using the initials W. G. F., but that seemed a mite too pretentious to the mountain men with whom he lived these days.

"Reckon that's right. I figure keeping to a straight line will bring us to Fort Union in three or four days."

Stromberg nodded his head in agreement. "It is true. We are still two weeks out, and that's barring accidents, sandbars, cranky boilers, and a hundred other possible mishaps."

Kit inclined his head toward the river. "Watkin and the others pulled out early."

"Good riddance, is all I have to say. I know their type well enough. I'm an old keelboatman myself, you know. In my younger days I helped push a keelboat up this river with Mike Fink and his band. A rough lot they were."

"Keep a wary eye out for them on your journey, Captain," Kit advised.

"We will do that. I've got me a scrappy crew who can fend for themselves. Why, even young Mr. LaBarge here has had his share of Indian fighting. A few river pirates should be short work for you, eh, Mr. LaBarge?"

The young pilot chuckled and said, "We won't need to fight them, Captain. The *Zenith* can easily outrun those old, lumbering barges."

Stromberg grinned. "You see, Mr. Carson? If we do have to keep an eye on those renegades, it will be an eye cast over our shoulders and past the *Zenith*'s stern as they fight against her wake. Well, good luck to you and your friend." The captain and his pilots trudged up the gangplank.

Kit continued down to solid ground and angled for the place where Gray Feather was taking his morning coffee. The Ute saw him coming and immediately stood and started over. Kit was afraid he was going to have to convince him all over again, but before the two men met, Jerome Heath interposed himself between them.

"Mr. Carson," he said with deep concern etched into his face.

"What is it, Mr. Heath?"

"It's Charlotte. Have you seen her this morning?"

"No."

"I can't find her anywhere. I checked her cabin,

but she wasn't there. No one has seen her."

"Have you asked Captain Stromberg?"

"No, I was just on my way to see him when I spied you. I thought that perhaps you had seen her."

"The last I saw of Miss Heath was when she went to her cabin last night."

Jerome chewed his lower lip worriedly, his eyes darting around the camp. "I'm at a loss as to what to do. We will be leaving shortly."

Hamner, who had strolled up with Gray Feather, was suddenly staring out across the river. "Say, you don't think them river pirates could have had anything to do with it?"

Heath's face instantly went slack, his complexion suddenly drained of all color. "My God! You don't think that scoundrel, Watkin, crept into her cabin during the night and took her!"

Kit had no way of knowing. All he *did* know was that he had heard nothing during the night. But considering how soundly he had slept on that civilized bed Stromberg had given him, there was no telling what he might have missed.

Some of the boat's hands came over to learn what the problem was, and before long the entire crew had gathered around. No one remembered seeing Charlotte that morning. Her kidnapping by Watkin and his crew was looking grimly possible.

"They couldn't have gotten very far," Kit said, starting for his horse. He snatched his saddle from the ground and threw it atop the tall dun. "I'll ride north and see if I can spot her on one of those boats."

Stromberg ordered LaBarge to hurry to the pilothouse and bring Kit the boat's spyglass.

"I'll have a head of steam up when you get back," Stromberg promised. "If they've taken her, we shall give chase at once! I'll run those scows off of this river!"

Kit shoved a moccasin into the stirrup and swung up onto his animal. Turning the horse away, he heeled its flanks and lunged into motion, but no sooner had he started off than he suddenly drew rein and brought the anxious animal to a halt. Kit stood in the stirrups and peered off to the west, then slowly lowered back to the seat. He turned his horse and walked it back.

"What's the matter?" Gray Feather asked.

Kit grinned and pointed to the rise of land a few hundred yards offshore. "Thar comes the wayward girl now, with her arms full of flowers, strolling along as if she hasn't a care in the world."

A moment later, Charlotte appeared atop the ridge exactly where Kit had predicted she would. Jerome Heath rushed to meet his daughter and ushered her back into camp. He wore a stern face as he reprimanded her, but he was obviously relieved that she had only been off collecting flowers and had not been kidnapped by those river rogues.

Everyone gave a sigh of relief.

Kit said, "Looks to me like her daddy can't make up his mind if he should hug her to death or paddle her soundly for worrying everyone like she did."

"She's a bit old for paddling," Gray Feather noted.

Kit laughed.

"Are you sure you won't change your mind, Kit?" Gray Feather persisted one last time as the

Zenith's big paddle wheels began to turn, slowly backing the steamer away from the river's bank and into deeper water. "We still can hail her back."

"I already told you how much time we'll save by going overland."

"Since when did saving time ever matter to you when there was adventure to be had? How often do we get a chance to ride upriver on a steamboat?"

"The few hours that I done it were enough. But if you want to go along, whal, I reckon I can wait for you up at Fort Union."

"What? And let you cross Blackfoot country all by yourself?"

Kit raised an arm and waved good-bye to Charlotte and Jerome Heath, who where standing at the promenade's handrail.

"There goes our chance," Gray Feather lamented as the steamer reversed her paddles and began chugging up against the current, gaining speed.

"Thar'll be more steamboat rides. I got a feeling that not too many years from now steamers will be puffing all up and down this here muddy creek."

The *Zenith* rounded a bend, and in a few minutes all that was left of her was a trail of smoke rising into the brilliant blue sky from behind the green bluffs. The air grew quiet, the way Kit liked it, and in some odd, unexplainable way, he felt a weight lift from his chest. Did technology really unnerve him that much? He had readily switched from using a flintlock rifle to a percussion rifle when they came along. That was technology, and he'd slipped into it as comfortably as a hand into a worn glove. So what was different here? Or was it just a fear of those loud, clattering engines fed from steam tanks that had a bad habit of blowing up on you?

"Reckon if we're going to do it on horseback, then we'd better start riding," Gray Feather said, resigned to his fate. His words pulled Kit from his thoughts.

"Reckon so."

"At least we've been fortunate to not have run across any Blackfeet."

"That we have," Kit mumbled, turning his horses away from the river.

No sooner had Kit spoken than the pleasant stillness was shattered. From behind them the air was suddenly filled with hideous war cries. The yelling merged with the thunder of pounding hooves.

Kit swiveled in his saddle. His heart leaped when he saw dozens of Blackfoot warriors charging down from the higher prairie toward the river bottom. Fear held them both ramrod straight in their saddles for a split second, then Kit shouted, "Ride for your life, Gray Feather!"

Yanking their horses about, the two trappers buried their heels and burst into a gallop.

Chapter Six

Kit's big horse stretched out beneath him, its long legs reaching as it flew across the ground. Gray Feather's smaller Indian pony was scrambling to keep up, but the stout pony was agile as a cat and moved with such fluid ease that one might suspect that horse and rider were one, like the centaur of ancient myth.

Behind them the Blackfeet began firing their rifles. Kit lay low against his horse's neck and urged him on to greater speed. The shoreline sped past on his right, and when a copse of cottonwood trees suddenly rose before them, Kit and Gray Feather veered up the steep embankment, momentarily losing sight of the river. When he chanced a glance over his shoulder the Blackfeet were still in hot pursuit, although they had not gained any ground on the fleeing trappers.

The trees thinned out, and ahead Kit could see the river again. The plume of smoke from the *Zenith* was much nearer now. A few more shots rang out behind them, but soon the Indians had emptied their rifles. Kit chanced another look over his shoulder. He had the impression that there was something wrong, but he didn't know what it could be. The Blackfeet were whooping and waving their weapons, and at the same time they seemed to be reeling oddly in their saddles, as if having some difficulty keeping an even keel.

The Indians' rifle shots had gone wide of their targets, but they had served one good purpose. They had alerted the riverboat up ahead, and as Kit and Gray Feather flailed their horses' flanks, Kit saw the boat heave toward the west bank. He could just make out the men swarming to her top deck.

"Make for the shore!" Kit shouted, angling his mount back toward the Missouri River.

The river loomed nearer. The *Zenith* was barreling under full steam now into the riverbank. Gray Feather's sturdy little mount had pulled slightly ahead of Kit, and it looked as though they would make the riverboat before the Blackfeet gained any ground on them. Upon the *Zenith*'s main deck, crewmen were already moving the gangplank into place in anticipation of making landfall.

Suddenly Gray Feather's mount broke stride and stumbled as if its hoof had hit a prairie dog hole. Scrambling, the horse tried to regain its stride, but instead went to its knees, flinging Gray Feather over its head.

It happened so fast that Kit was already fifty

yards beyond the kicking animal by the time he was able to pull his own mount to a halt. Kit wheeled about and charged back. Gray Feather was struggling to his hands and knees, shaking his head as if dazed.

Seeing that fate had dropped the two trappers into their hands, the Blackfeet raised their voices and spread out to encircle them.

"You all right?" Kit said, reining to a halt beside his friend.

"I . . . I don't know," Gray Feather stammered, clutching his rifle and staggering to his feet.

Kit buried his rifle against his shoulder and took a bead on one of the swiftly approaching warriors. He touched the trigger, and the rifle barked. A hundred yards away one of the warriors yelped and flipped backward off his horse. Kit reached for Gray Feather's arm and swung his partner onto the dun. By now the Blackfeet were closing in on all sides.

Kit spun around once, twice, then, narrowing an eye at the only avenue of escape open to them, he kicked his horse into motion. He had lost valuable seconds rescuing his friend, and now the Blackfeet were nearly on them. . . .

The crackle of rifles erupted from the deck of the *Zenith,* dropping three Indians in the initial hail of bullets. Kit angled for the riverboat, driving his animal hard even as the ramp was being shoved out onto the shore. Hardly slowing down at all, he pounded up the gangplank and onto the waiting boat.

"Full reverse!" he heard Captain Stromberg's voice bellow from the pilothouse above him. The staccato crack of gunfire sounded like Independence Day! Kit and Gray Feather leaped from the horse, wrapping the reins of the nervous animal around the timbers supporting the second deck. Diving for cover, Kit swiftly reloaded his rifle.

The paddles began their powerful backward rotation, but nothing happened. The boat remained stubbornly in place where its nose had plowed into the muddy bank.

Rifle fire from the high ground along the shore rained back at them. A bullet splintered a railing near Kit. He narrowed an eye along the barrel of his rifle and squeezed the trigger.

Gray Feather had crawled behind some barrels. His rifle barked, and up on the beach a Blackfoot spun around and scrambled for cover on all fours. Overhead the barrage from the upper deck was taking its toll as the Blackfeet dived for cover, making only hastily aimed shots.

But the Indians held the high ground, and they had the advantage as long as the *Zenith* remained mired in place.

"More power to the engines," Stromberg ordered through the pounding and the clanking and the gunfire. Kit had taken a position near the larboard-side paddle box, and as he rammed another ball down the barrel of his rifle it appeared to him that the big paddle wheel was churning up solid mud instead of water. A brown plum had begun to spread like a bloody wound all around the stranded vessel.

Kit glimpsed a flash arcing through the sky from the shoreline, and the next instant a flaming arrow thumped into a canvas-covered pile of crates nearby. He wrenched the arrow from the tarpaulin and beat out the fire with his hat. Two more fiery arrows dropped in, both burying themselves somewhere in the deck overhead.

As the battle raged, crewmen ran forward carrying long poles. They thrust the poles into the muddy waters and leaned into them with all their weight, their muscles bulging and straining as they tried to shove the boat off the mud. Kit felt the *Zenith* budge and slip backward a few feet. Another burning arrow traced an arc across a sky clouded with gun smoke and thumped into the deck. Immediately a crewman plucked it out and threw it overboard.

One of the pole men threw up his arms and lurched backward, sprawled spread-eagle onto the deck with a red spot blooming on his shirt. Kit leaped for the pole before it slipped into the water and, leaning into it, added his strength to that of the others.

A man cried out overhead; a moment later, a body crashed to the deck at Kit's feet.

Slowly the boat began to move, then, suddenly breaking free, it shuddered and strove backward, gaining speed. Once loose of the clinging mud, the steamer's engines began thumping like fire-breathing monsters, the wheels revolving freely, water splashing and drumming inside the paddle boxes. In a few seconds they were out of range of the Indians' arrows, but not their rifles.

As the shoreline receded, the gunfire from that quarter became more sporadic until finally, as the riverboat made the middle of the Missouri, it stopped altogether. The boat reversed her engines and met the challenge of the current head-on, plowing up the wide stream. Kit drew in the pole and set it on the deck. Captain Stromberg was shouting down orders to the engineer from the pilothouse on top of the boat.

The *Zenith* was a bundle of activity. Kit stepped out of the way as men dashed about, tending the wounded, stamping out small fires, inspecting the pipes and ducts and other bent and shining pieces of metal, the purpose of which Kit had no idea.

From the shoreline an occasional shot rang out, reminding everyone aboard that they were still not out of danger. Kit stood at the fenders near the paddle box and watched the Blackfeet hurrying to their horses and mounting up.

Gray Feather stood up from behind the barrels and came over.

"You all right, pard?" Kit asked.

"I am. Thanks for coming back for me, Kit."

"Shoot, you'd have done so for me."

"That was a close one." Gray Feather shook his head ruefully. "I regret losing my horse. He was a good stallion."

"He did shine," Kit agreed, "but look at it this way—you're back on this here riverboat, just like you wanted to be."

"Yes, but I think I'd have preferred a more dignified arrival."

Kit laughed. "I'm going up top to talk to Stromberg."

"I'll go to the engine room. I saw Mr. Hamner looking kind of concerned. I hope the engines haven't been damaged."

Kit frowned. "I could have gone all day without you saying that, Gray Feather."

"Look at you. You hardly bat an eye when you escape a Blackfoot war party by the skin of your teeth, and nearly get yourself shot trying to push this boat off the muddy bottom. But when I mention steam engines, you suddenly look as if you've just been invited to tea with old Beelzebub."

"Whal, you can fancy up to that wheezing bucket of steam if you like, Gray Feather. As for me, I'd just as soon welcome a couple of Yellow Wolf's Cheyenne dog soldiers into my lodge. Leastwise with Injuns I know the way the stick floats. These new contraptions are beyond most men's ken, and I ain't too proud to admit that I don't understand 'em, and I don't trust 'em."

"You'll change your mind one of these days when you see how perfectly safe they are."

"Uh-huh. The same day I decide a serpent is a fit traveling companion." Kit left the Ute there and climbed the staircases to the top deck, where he found Captain Stromberg standing by the railing with a long spyglass to his eye, watching the Blackfeet scrambling for their horses.

"Mr. Carson," he said when Kit walked over. "That was a close call. I'm glad we were able to get you and your friend out of their clutches."

"Gray Feather and I appreciate it, but you nearly lost your boat in the effort."

"It was close. But I have found that just living from day to day in this wilderness involves risk and chance, sir." Stromberg put the glass back to his eye and pointed it at the shore again, frowning. "Craziest damned thing I ever did see. By all rights you and Mr. Smith should have been dead by now."

"I reckon the Almighty was looking out for us."

"Hmm. I wonder. Do you know Indians very well, Mr. Carson?"

"Know 'em?"

"Yes. Understand them? Their ways?"

"Reckon I know them as well as any white man in these parts."

"Hmm. Curious."

"What is?"

"Those crazy savages are acting . . . well . . . peculiar. Here, have a look for yourself. What do you make of it?"

Kit put the piece to his eye and brought the distant shoreline into clear focus. Most of the Blackfeet were still gathering up their animals. Some had already mounted up and were riding along the riverbank as if looking for a place to fire upon the riverboat when she passed by. The others seemed to be having considerable trouble walking. At first Kit thought they were the wounded left behind, but on closer scrutiny he discovered that they weren't wounded at all. Some staggered this way and that as if not certain where they should be going. One Indian swung up onto his horse, only to slide off the other side. As Kit watched in amazement, he was certain that the fellow who had fallen was sitting upon the ground giggling!

Another rider was galloping north with the others, reeling side to side upon his pony.

"See what I mean?" Stromberg said.

All at once Kit understood, and it explained everything, including how he and Gray Feather had managed to outrun them and how the Indians' bullets had gone so far of target. Kit lowered the spyglass and shook his head.

"They aren't crazy, Captain. Them Injuns are falling-down drunk!"

"Drunk?" Stromberg roared out, laughing.

"Drunk as rats in a monastery's cellar."

Stromberg's whiskers rippled as he chuckled. "I say you owe your escape to a few pints of ale." He chuckled again. "Like it or not, it looks like you're stuck with us for a few more miles at least."

Kit frowned. "What with Gray Feather afoot now, it looks like we're stuck for the whole trip."

"Captain?"

Stromberg turned as Engineer John Hamner and Gray Feather came across the deck from the staircase. Both men wore downturned faces, and that made Kit's skin crawl.

"We got trouble, sir."

"What sort of trouble, Mr. Hamner?"

"It's that fight we put up trying to get off the mud."

"Were the engines harmed?"

"The engines are just fine, but in giving them all the pressure we could generate I had to open the intake valves all the way."

Stromberg understood immediately. "I see. How bad is it?"

"We're creeping into the yellow."

"Hmm." Sudden concern dragged down the lines of the captain's face. "Well, we can't do anything about it until we've put some distance between us and those Indians along the shore. Can you nurse them along for a while?"

"I can if we throttle her back to a crawl. But we won't be making much headway against this current."

"Well, do what you have to. Soon as we shake those Indians we'll put in to shore and see to the matter."

"Right, Captain." Hamner spun about on his

heel and hurried back down the steps.

"What's the trouble?" Kit asked.

"Oh, it's nothing to concern yourself with, Mr. Carson. We seem to have filled our boilers with mud again, that's all. This damned river! Well, as soon as we shake our friends on shore we'll heave to and clean them out . . . *again*!"

"Nothing to concern myself with!" Kit said after the captain had left to investigate the matter. He looked up sharply at Gray Feather. "This boat is about to blow you, me, and everyone on it clear to the moon, and he says it's nothing to concern myself with!"

Gray Feather only grimaced and shrugged his shoulders. "I'm sure that if they thought that was likely they'd shut the engines down immediately."

Kit snatched his rifle from where he had leaned it against the handrail and started off.

"Where are you going?"

"Down to them boilers to keep an eye peeled on that needle myself. If it gets to tickling that thar red line and them boilers commence to wailing, I'm making for open water fast as these hoofs of mine can carry me!"

Kit winced when a random rifle shot from the shore rang out. The river had narrowed some and was narrowing even further ahead. It was not beyond possibility that the Blackfeet's bullets could still hit passengers or crew, or cause some damage to the machinery.

Kit cast an impatient eye at the Indians paralleling the riverboat on horseback and said disgustedly, "Got Bug's Boys on one side of me and a pot of steam under my tail big enough to make Old Hickory's cannon look like popguns! Wagh!

Gray Feather, the next time I get a wild hair to go and take a gallivant to someplace where I don't need to be, I hope you sit this child down and talk some sense into him!" Kit glanced at Stromberg's spyglass, which he still held. "Here, you keep an eye on the Blackfeet while I go down and keep an eye on this here boat."

With his long rifle swinging in his fist at his side, Kit hiked down the steps.

Frowning, Gray Feather turned back to the railing, extended the spyglass, and trained it on the drunken swarm of Indians racing along the Missouri's bank. In spite of their intoxicated condition, they were easily keeping up with the riverboat, which was barely creeping along now under half power.

Chapter Seven

Watkin lowered the spyglass and grinned.

"Well, what's all the shooting about?"

Watkin glanced over at Smitter. The two men were atop one of the bluffs where the Missouri River pinched in. Below them in a bend, beyond the view of the approaching riverboat, lay both their keelboats, one on each side of the river. Smitter and a couple of his men had come over from the *Warrior* on the skiff. "It's Eagle-head and his boys. They've got that riverboat on the run."

"Lemme see." Smitter put the long lens to his eye, scrunching the other shut. "What's wrong with them Injuns, anyway?" he asked after studying the scene unfolding a mile downriver.

"Offhand, I'd say the chief and his boys are drunk."

"That's just wonderful," Smitter growled in disgust. "Now what are we to do? We'll have to change our plans, and we better do it right quick!" He cast a worried eye down at the river where their boats were tied up. At that distance the thick cordelling rope that had been stretched across the river from each boat's bow was hardly visible.

"Change them? Hmm. I wonder . . . ?"

"What's that I'm hearing in your voice, Watkin?"

The sandy-haired river pirate thought a moment. "Why change them? In fact, Eagle-head and his warriors might be a big help to us."

Smitter narrowed an eye suspiciously. "What are you thinking?"

"You saw what that riverboat was carrying. Enough whiskey to keep every savage in the territory drunk for a month. And the guns, too. If we can haul that steamer to a stop and drive her into shore, we can patch up hard feelings with Eagle-head by handing out some of that cargo. In return we can do with the crew and passengers as we see fit and take the lion's share of what that boat is carrying farther upriver to the Yellowstone and do some trading with the Crow and Sioux. On our way back we might even hit the Mandans and Rees. We'll float into St. Louis with enough furs to make even the big companies stand up and take notice!"

"Notice? Not too close a notice, I hope," Smitter added ominously. "Don't want folks asking questions about how we come by so much fur."

Watkin laughed. "You fret too much, my friend. We'll use all our usual precautions. Besides, the men we trade with aren't in the business of asking questions. They're in the business of making money."

The two captains scrambled down the dusty bluff back to the keelboat. Israel Copp asked what all the shooting was about when Watkin and Smitter stepped back aboard the *River Maid*. Watkin told the men what they had seen and the twist it had put in their plans.

Smitter and his men took the rowboat back across the river where he and his crew would wait for the *Zenith* to round the bend. When she came into view, the *Warrior* and the *River Maid* would immediately move apart, stretching the cordelling ropes taut across the river. If all worked as planned, they'd snag the steamer in midstream, board her, overpower her crew, and run her aground.

With Eagle-head's help, there would be little resistance.

As the two keelboats readied themselves, Watkin was thinking not only of the booty they were about to seize, but about the fair-haired beauty who had spurned him in front of that trapper, Carson.

He grinned to himself and checked the pistols thrust under his belt. He had special plans for both Carson and the girl once this was over.

"They won't keep it up very long," Captain Stromberg surmised hopefully as he stood beneath the boiler deck, peering out at the whooping riders galloping along the shore. At that moment the Blackfeet were not much more than a hundred yards away. The narrowing river and a sandbar that stretched out from the river's east bank had forced the riverboat in closer to shore. It could not be helped. They were driving up a chute toward two high bluffs that flanked the river on either side. Here snags were particularly bothersome, and the pilot was doing an admirable job of avoiding them.

Beneath the boiler deck, where presently most of the activity was going on, was the ship's huge black furnaces supporting their iron cylinders of high-pressure steam. Kit was keeping an eye on the pressure gauge, which still gave a reading just below that of "impending doom," hovering somewhere instead at about the "sweating anxiety" level.

Finally admitting to himself that he could be of little help here, and that he was only getting in the way of Hamner's efforts to keep the raging beast under control, Kit temporarily gave up his vigil and stepped to the captain's side. A smattering of rifle fire from the shore had begun to come into the boat, spitting splinters of wood here and there. No one had been hit by this renewed effort, but it was bothersome enough to keep everyone scurrying about in a crouch and sticking to the starboard side of the boat whenever possible.

From up on the top deck a few rifle shots answered those coming in from the river's bank. The crewmen up there were better marksmen—or perhaps it was simply that they were all stone sober and had a stable platform to shoot from. In any event, two Blackfeet reeled from their animals. The others angled farther west, and for a moment the sporadic bullets stopped thudding into the *Zenith*. This was of some relief to Kit, for he had no idea what effect an errant hunk of lead smashing into one of the boilers might have on it.

Kit said to Stromberg, "When Injuns see that

they're grappling with the short end of a stick, they generally let go. They don't stick around when the odds begin to weigh again' them, Captain."

"I was hoping that might be so, Mr. Carson." Stromberg stepped out onto one of the boat's fenders, grabbed a hog chain, and leaned out to peer upriver. "Once we're past those narrows, the river widens and becomes deeper. With any luck these heathens will have given up on their chase and we can put in to the far shore to make our repairs."

Charlotte's face appeared around the corner from the starboard side of the boat. "Captain Stromberg," she shouted past the roaring furnaces, where crewmen busily tossed lengths of firewood into the gaping maws. If Kit had learned anything at all about riverboats—aside from the disturbing fact that they tended to blow up on you—it was that they consumed a horrendous amount of wood. Fuel stops were regular and frequent, and Kit suspected that if steam travel ever caught on along this river, soon the entire Missouri River shore would be as barren of wood as the Sahara.

The two men crossed the sixty-foot-wide deck to the starboard side, where the *Zenith*'s bulk protected them from the sporadic rifle fire.

"Yes, Miss Heath?" Stromberg asked.

She glanced worriedly from him to Kit and said, "I am pleased you weren't injured by those Indians, Mr. Carson."

"You and me both, ma'am," he agreed. Her hair was scattered, with long reddish-brown strands spilling down her forehead and over her cheek.

Two buttons of the high neck of her dress had been ripped off. Her face was smudged, and blood streaked the material of her dress. In a flash her eyes darted back toward Stromberg and she said, "I have had the wounded all brought into the main cabin. There are six men. Another three are dead, I am sorry to say."

"I appreciate you taking on the task, Miss Heath. I'm sure the men will be in good hands."

There was nothing at the moment that Kit could do to help with the boat, so he offered his services to Charlotte. "I've had some dealing with bullet wounds, ma'am."

"Thank you for your offer. I can use all the help I can get. I've started heating water, and with the captain's permission, I'd like to take some sheets for bandages."

"By all means, Miss Heath."

Kit followed Charlotte along the main deck to the stairs leading up to the second deck—the boiler deck—so named, Kit reckoned, because it was built above the boilers. On their way, they ran into a worried-looking Warren Randle coming from the other direction. His plaid vest hung open and his ample stomach pressed at the dingy, sweat-soaked shirt beneath it. He carried a new rifle, one recently appropriated from the supplies bound for Fort Union, Kit suspected.

"Where's Stromberg?" he barked as Kit and Charlotte approached. "That man will have hell to pay if any of the company's stores fall into the hands of those savages!"

"Stromberg is busy seeing to it that those boilers don't blow us all to kingdom come. You ever care for a man with a bullet wound?"

"No."

"Whal, then I'll show you how it's done." Kit grabbed Randle's vest and tugged him along. Randle blustered in protest as Kit turned him up the stairs and shoved him along. "Your company stores will be all right so long as them engines don't commence to having conniption fits. And if you go bothering the captain now, that's just what's likely to happen."

Randle tried to break free of Kit's grasp. "Just who do you think you are, Carson? You can't order me around. My company is paying for this boat!"

"I'm second cousin to a grizzly b'ar and ornery as a badger gone to ground. And that's when I'm in a friendly mood. Right now I'm strung tighter than a fiddle, and if you value your scalp, Mr. Randle, you'll settle down and give Miss Heath a hand with the wounded. Your company's stores don't happen to include bandages and iodine tinctures, do they?"

"No."

"Too bad." Kit thrust the clerk through the doorway of the main cabin. Inside, wounded men had been lain out upon the floor. They were being looked after by a couple of the crew members, but none appeared as if he knew what he was doing, especially Jerome Heath, who stood off to one side of the long room, mouth agape and flushed about the gills.

Kit made a quick survey of the wounds. Four men bore only superficial injuries, which required only cleaning and bandaging; they would keep until the boat was out of harm's way. Three of the men were more seriously wounded, however, and they needed immediate attention. Kit called for the kettle of warm water that Charlotte had put on the stove and shoved a bedsheet into Randle's hands. "Rip this into strips."

"You have no right—" Randle groused, but gulped back the rest of what he was about to say when Kit lanced him with a pointed stare.

The door opened and Marcus Williams and his partner came through. "Can me and Oscar help here?" Williams asked.

"You ever tend to a bullet wound?"

"No, but Oscar was in the war."

"That's right, Mr. Carson. I've seen plenty of shot-up men before. I'm no surgeon but I'll do what I can."

"We got to stop the bleeding first. That fellow over there, and the one by the stove, are in a real bad way. Do for them first."

Marcus and Oscar lent a hand where they could. Randle reluctantly tore up sheets. Charlotte brought over the kettle of hot water. The low groans of hurting men turned the narrow room into a depressing place in spite of the sunlight streaming through the windows. But Kit and the others were too busy to take notice.

A shadow cast itself across the boat. Kit glanced out the window at the tall bluffs rising immediately to his left. They would be passing into wider water, according to what Captain Stromberg had told him, once they were past the bluffs. Then they would be able to pull into the far bank and see to the wounded men and the ship's boilers.

Kit felt a vague wave of relief at seeing that landmark drift slowly past.

But it was a short-lived reprieve.

Almost at once a voice outside shouted a warning from the deck above them. Kit could not make out the words. Something about a snag . . . or a trap?

Then the *Zenith* gave a violent shudder. Somewhere at her bow wood started to groan like a woman in labor. Everyone in the cabin lurched forward. Kit clutched at the wounded man he was tending while at he same time he reached for Charlotte, who had just stood.

Had they rammed into another sunken sandbar?

With a crack like a gunshot, the jackstaff at the boat's bow snapped, folding back on itself and smashing the railing of the promenade. The boat lurched forward a few dozen feet before being drawn down nearly to a halt.

From outside near the prow someone gave a sudden cry of alarm. Wood shrieked and cargo tumbled freely. Kit leaped for the door, steadied himself at the doorjamb, then plunged outside to see what it was they had run into.

Chapter Eight

At first he could see nothing amiss other than the broken jackstaff at the *Zenith*'s bow, and a pile of cargo that had once been neatly stacked but was now scattered about as if a giant had reached out and swatted it.

Yet the boat had definitely drawn down to a crawl. It had collided with something, but what?

Kit's eyes shot to the bluffs. The Indians had reined to a halt and were watching something upon the water. Kit took another look and finally spotted the heavy rope that was stretched across the steamer. It hadn't been there when Kit had come forward from the boilers a few minutes before. He was perplexed. Then movement caught his eye, and when he looked across the river he spotted one of the keelboats sliding swiftly into the river. The second boat appeared an instant later from the opposite side of the river, gliding so quickly that it might have been under steam power itself. . . .

Suddenly Kit realized the truth!

The rope was attached to both keelboats, and it was the *Zenith* that was towing these crafts along. And Kit noticed something else, too. The natural movement of the riverboat was swinging both keelboats into her gunwales!

Aboard the *Warrior* and *River Maid* the river pirates were hauling in the rope, drawing the keelboats toward the *Zenith*. The rope had to be cut! Kit yanked his butcher knife from its sheath, but before he could take a step a boom thundered across the river from the *River Maid*'s deck cannon. The ball cut through a supporting timber and the corner of the deck where Kit stood erupted in splinters.

Leaping back from the gaping hole that had suddenly opened up, Kit saw a crewman below scrambling over the scattered cargo with a blade in his fist. Rifle fire from both keelboats began to rain in. The man reached the rope, but before he could cut it a bullet stopped him, knocking him down among the barrels and crates.

"Cut that line!" Stromberg's voice boomed from somewhere below. The captain appeared by the stricken man. He grabbed up the knife and dove for the line. But before he could reach it he, too, spun around and staggered back, clutching his shoulder.

Kit dove back into the main cabin for his rifle. Outside, he drew a bead on one of the keelboats and knocked a pirate off of its cabin's roof.

The cannon boomed a second time, crumpling

one of the tall chimneys overhead. With a screech of twisting metal, the long black tube crashed to the deck. Smoke poured through the new opening.

Swiftly reloading, Kit steadied the rifle on the man at the cannon and fired. The pirate flipped back and disappeared into the muddy Missouri. Immediately another man took his place. Kit spilled gunpowder down the barrel of his rifle and chased it with a patched ball. Thumbing a percussion cap onto the nipple, he swung the rifle toward the front of the riverboat and narrowed an eye at the rope there.

Gunfire erupted all across the river as the pirates fired on the riverboat and Stromberg's crew returned the favor. More rifle fire had begun to come from the bluffs as the Indians, apparently bolstered by the pirates' attack, resumed their own attack on the riverboat.

Kit put the melee out of mind and concentrated on the rope, steadying his sights on it as his finger folded into the trigger guard. Then Watkin's keelboat slammed into the *Zenith*'s starboard gunwale, pitching her sideways. Kit's finger touched the trigger at that very moment and his shot went wide.

The *Zenith* trembled again as the second keelboat slammed into her larboard gunwale. Pirates swarmed aboard, and the heavy reports of rifles gave way to the sharper cracks of pistols as the fighting moved into close quarters.

Two pirates scrambled up the stairs. Kit crouched back around the corner, and as they came through the main cabin's doorway he greeted the first one with the curved iron butt plate of his rifle. The man staggered back into the arms of his partner, his mouth instantly flowing red. He'd be gumming his steak from now on, Kit mused as he swung the rifle around and cracked the second fellow's skull.

Both men crumpled to the deck.

Kit leaped over their bodies and plunged down the stairs, trading his rifle for a tomahawk. Turning a corner, he backpedaled when one of the pirates suddenly barred his way, a pistol leveled at Kit's gut. Instantly Kit threw himself against one of the support timbers and slashed down with his tomahawk, cutting into the pistol's wooden stock as its hammer dropped, spraying smoke and sparks and a bullet that just missed his thigh. Kit followed through with a left jab, and finished him off with a sweeping blow from the flat of the ax's blade against the pirate's temple.

A glance showed him that the battle was going against the riverboat's crew. The *Zenith* was still chugging up the river, but at a snail's pace now with the two keelboats in tow. Kit had to cut it free! Wheeling back around toward the bow, he fought past another pirate, then his way was clear to the rope. Seizing the opportunity, Kit raised the tomahawk high for a single blow to the rope.

Something hard smacked into his head from behind. His teeth rattled at the impact and his brain exploded with millions of bright, blinding lights shooting into the back of his eyes like Chinese fountains . . . and that was the last thing Kit remembered until hours later.

Watkin lowered the rifle and looked at the crumpled form at his feet. Then he laughed.

"That's just the beginning, Carson. When I'm done with you you'll rue the day you ever decided to stick your nose into my business."

Israel Copp ran up along the main deck from the larboard paddle box where the last stronghold of Captain Stromberg's crew were holding out, falling one by one beneath Watkin and Smitter's superior numbers. "The boat's ours!" Copp declared. "Got the engineer as he was about to jump overboard and two or three others. Most of everyone else is down."

"What about the pilot?"

"Pilot's dead. But we got his cub. We found that girl and her father, too. They're up in the main cabin with some of the wounded."

"Good. Take the ones still on their feet to the main cabin."

"What about this one?" Copp asked, glancing down at Kit.

"He'll have a whopper of a headache when he wakes up. I have special plans for him, and for that Indian partner of his. Is he among the captives?"

"He is."

"Good. There's a room back there where we can lock them up until I'm ready to deal with them."

"You will answer to the law for what you have done, Watkin!" Captain Stromberg growled, standing up among the scattered cargo, clutching his wounded shoulder.

"Ah! Captain," Watkin replied, grinning. "I am disappointed to see you still alive. I'm a better shot than that. The boat must have pitched at the moment I pulled the trigger."

"What is the meaning of this, you scoundrel?"

"Meaning? Why, isn't it obvious? I'm taking over your boat and all that she carries."

"You'll not get away with it."

"Who is to stop me? Who within a thousand miles of us is there to say I can't do exactly as I please, Captain Stromberg?"

"By God—"

"It will do you little good to invoke the deity, Captain. You see, on this river I am the Almighty. At least at the moment." Watkin laughed again and turned to Copp. "Take the captain and Carson out of here. Then let's figure out how to turn this boat in to shore."

"You'll not get away with this," Stromberg roared as two pirates jumped to do Watkin's bidding and dragged the fuming captain away.

Watkin climbed the splintered steps to the second deck and went through the doorway to the main cabin, where a half-dozen of the keelboat pirates had the few survivors under heavy guard.

"The lovely Miss Heath," he said, bowing at the waist. "You don't know what a pleasure it is to see you again." He frowned. "Too bad the circumstances aren't more pleasant."

"What will you do with us?"

"You, my dear, I only intend to make happy. The others, if they behave themselves, I might allow to live."

"You wouldn't!"

"I love the way your eyes spark when you are angry."

Charlotte raised a fist, but a river pirate snagged her wrist before she could pummel Watkin's broad chest.

"Control yourself, my dear. We shall have plenty

of time this evening to discuss the matter." Watkin looked at the faces of the men held captive there. "You," he said, singling out LaBarge. "You're a pilot?"

"I am," LaBarge said, standing away from one of the wounded men he'd been comforting.

"Come with me." He put a pistol against the young man's spine and guided him out the doorway and up to the pilothouse. The place was a wreck; shattered glass crunched beneath their boots, the brass speaking tube that rose up from the floor had been peppered with three bullet holes, and some of the polished spokes of the helm were splintered. Gunderson Moore's body lay sprawled on the floor where a bullet through the head had dropped him instantly.

"Run her into the shore up ahead there," Watkin ordered.

"I'll need an engineer to man the engines."

"Do without," he said.

LaBarge frowned. "Whatever you say." Taking the big wheel in hand, he spun it around and clamped it down with a foot on a spoke where it passed through the floor. The riverboat heeled over and made for the shore, looming closer and closer until forty feet away the big boat ground into the gravel and mud and trembled to a stop, its powerful paddles thrashing the water to no avail.

"This is as far as she's going, Mr. Watkin," LaBarge informed him.

"It's far enough. Now, back down with the others."

"Someone ought to shut down the engines," LaBarge said.

"All in due time," Watkin chirped. He was suddenly in fine spirits. He'd captured the *Zenith* and all that she carried. Now he had only one last problem to overcome. He looked to the riverbank where Chief Eagle-head and his warriors were gathering. Watkin returned LaBarge to the main cabin, jumped overboard into the knee-deep water, and he and eight of his men waded ashore.

"Chief Eagle-head," he said pleasantly, raising a hand in friendship. "I saw from the bluff that you had some desire for this boat, so I figured I'd lend a hand."

"Watkin. You cheated Eagle-head!"

"Cheated? Whatever are you talking about?"

"No whiskey."

"No whiskey?" Watkin fixed a puzzled look to his face, then transferred it to the warriors, who were scowling back at them. "Whatever do you mean?"

"You give water in barrel. No whiskey. You cheated Eagle-head!"

"Your boys look to be right happily drunk, Chief. How could they get drunk on plain water?"

The chief called for one of his warriors to come forward. The man had somehow managed to carry the keg without tumbling from the saddle, a surprising feat considering he was half drunk, like the rest of the warriors. At a command from his chief, the Indian threw the keg at Watkin's feet, breaking it open. What spilled out, not surprisingly, was good old Missouri River water.

"Mr. Copp!" Watkin snapped after dipping a finger in it and taking a taste.

"Yes, Captain?" Copp said, confused.

"Wasn't it you who fetched this keg off the boat for the chief?"

"Er, well, yes it was."

Watkin looked totally appalled. "I trusted you to bring the chief a keg of whiskey, and look what you've done! You've brought disgrace on me and you've cheated the chief."

"But you said . . ."

Watkin drew a pistol from his belt and fired. Copp's head snapped back and he fell into the river. Slowly, Watkin lowered the gun. The other pirates stared in disbelief. Thrusting the weapon back under his belt, Watkin said, "Let that be a lesson to all of you who might think they can cheat our friends the Blackfeet!"

The Indians were staring in shocked disbelief too. Watkin said to the chief, "I'm sorry for you having been shorted on our trade, Chief Eaglehead. I take full responsibility." His contrite expression brightened a little, and he added, "But there is plenty of whiskey aboard the riverboat." He ordered two kegs brought ashore for the Blackfeet.

The Indians made camp there on the bank while Watkin had his men begin off-loading the *Zenith*'s cargo onto the *Warrior* and *River Maid*, which were still tied fast to the riverboat. After the display he had put on in front of the Blackfeet, not one of the pirates dared question Watkin's orders.

With evening coming on, Watkin returned to the main cabin where some of the crew were still being held. Stromberg, LaBarge, Hamner, Gray Feather, and Kit had been locked up in a small storage room under the boiler deck. Charlotte and her father, along with Warren Randle, Marcus Williams, and his partner, Oscar, were still in the main cabin with the wounded.

"How long do you intend to keep us locked up?" Jerome Heath demanded when Watkin made his appearance.

But before the pirate could answer him, Randle cut in, raging, "That is property of the American Fur Company you are handing out to those savages, I'll have you know. You'll have the devil to pay once Mr. Pratte and Mr. Chouteau find out what you have done."

"Get the little man out of here," Watkin barked.

"Where to?" one of the guards asked, grabbing Randle by the vest.

"Feed him to the catfish."

"No! Please!" Randle pleaded.

The guard hauled him out the door.

Everyone moved to the windows on the river side of the boat, where they could see the pirate wrestle the struggling clerk to the railing and, with the help of another man, heave him overboard. They heard the splash, saw Randle sputter back to the surface and stand in water to his waist.

Randle looked up at something the others could not see and suddenly cried out, "Noooo!" Covering his head with his arms, he plunged back under water as rifle shots rang out from the promenade.

Charlotte turned away from the window, terror draining the color from her face. Her father stepped to her side, draping a comforting arm over her trembling shoulder. "It's all right, darling" he said softly.

"It *will* be all right," Watkin said, "if you all do precisely as I say."

"What do you want of us?" Jerome Heath asked warily.

"Of you, nothing. Of your daughter?" He smiled

angelically, as if there were not a trace of deceit in his entire being. His eyes shifted to Charlotte's lovely face. "Only that she treats me with the respect that I deserve—that I demand!" he added with an un-angelic edge.

Charlotte started to speak, but the warning squeeze of her father's hand upon her shoulder silenced her.

"She is only an innocent child!" Heath answered with indignation.

"Innocent? What is innocence? I look at innocence as a jail cell holding a person against their will, and I consider it my duty to free one and all from its clutches." Watkin laughed and took Charlotte firmly by the arm. When she hesitated to come with him he said to his men, "Bring the father along."

Two men came alongside Jerome and clamped his arms tight.

"What do you want us to do with these others?" one of the remaining guards asked just before Watkin left.

"Throw the wounded overboard. We have no time to waste on them. I'll decide about the others later."

"No!" Charlotte pleaded.

"No?" Watkin grinned. "The lady doth protest?"

"Don't hurt them. I'll come with you, and I won't fight you."

"Ah! A bargain? Your affection for the worthless lives of these men?"

All Charlotte could do was avert her eyes and meekly nod her head.

"Very well. Let them live . . . for the moment, at least."

Watkin marched them down to the main deck, where Chief Eagle-head and some of his men were poking through the American Fur Company's supplies. The sun was nearly down and the river was darkening. Lights from the windows of the rocking keelboats cast their uneven light across the rippling water.

"Chief Eagle-head," Watkin said, finding the man with his head poked into a barrel.

The chief looked up. He was clutching a handful of red ribbons in one hand, and a brand-new J & S Hawkens rifle in the other. "Much good stuff," he said, grinning drunkenly and shaking the hand that held the ribbons. "Make Eagle-head much happy!"

"As it should be," Watkin concurred. "Will you help me?"

"Help you?"

"Would you have some of your warriors take this man ashore?" He indicated Jerome Heath. "Make sure he is tied up good and tight." Watkin shifted his view to Charlotte and held it there for a long moment. "Come morning I will decide what to do with him. Perhaps I shall allow him to live. But then again, perhaps I will give his scalp to you, Chief. It all depends . . ." He left that last thought unspoken, but his meaning was clear to everyone there.

Eagle-head grunted and said that he would do as Watkin asked.

A Blackfoot warrior carried a keg of whiskey past them to the gunwale and dropped it into the river where a second man fished it out and staggered ashore with it. Eagle-head relayed the request to the warrior, who roughly hauled Jerome along after him.

"Now," Watkin said, bending his elbow for Charlotte to thread her arm through, "come along with me, my dear."

With a grimace of distaste, Charlotte put her arm through Watkin's and went with him, past the leering and snickering men standing there, onto the *River Maid* and down into the keelboat's cabin.

Chapter Nine

Clawing his way up from the dark pit of nothingness, Kit struggled to regain consciousness. A wave of nausea swept over him, and he thought that he was going to be sick. But it passed. Slowly he became aware of the throbbing pain in the back of his head and the ache in his shoulder where he must have hit the deck when he was knocked unconscious. The deep thirst that thickened his tongue suggested to him that he had been unconscious for a long time.

In spite of himself, Kit let out a low groan. It was dangerous to make any noise when you had no idea where you were, or if you were alone. But it slipped out anyway, and there was nothing Kit could do to stop it.

"Kit!" It was Gray Feather's voice.

Kit opened his eyes and saw only more darkness. But now he was aware of movement and the low murmur of voices. He tried to sit up. A pair of hands reached out from the darkness and helped him.

"Where am I?"

"They locked us up in the aft boiler closet, under the boiler deck," another voice replied.

"Captain Stromberg?" The last Kit remembered, Stromberg had been shot down while trying to cut the keelboats free of the *Zenith*.

"Yes, it's me."

"I saw you take a bullet."

"A shoulder wound, is all," Stromberg answered tightly, clipping his words as if it was an effort to speak. Kit had been shot in the shoulder once, and he understood the pain. He also knew that afterward, all you wanted to do was remain quiet and hope that no one went poking around to see how badly hurt you really were.

Slowly Kit's eyes grew accustomed to the faint light coming through a tiny window high up in the wall. There were other men in the cramped closet as well. "Who else is here?"

"I'm here." That was young Joseph LaBarge's voice.

"Me too," Hamner replied.

"How about the others?"

Gray Feather said, "The rest of the passengers and the crew are locked up in the main cabin, Kit. Watkin has them under heavy guard."

"Why are we down here?"

Although he couldn't see Gray Feather's expression, he had the feeling the man was frowning. "Watkin says he has special plans for us. I don't know what that means, but I didn't much care for the glint in his eye when he gathered us together and locked us in here."

"What about Charlotte?" Kit asked.

No one knew anything. LaBarge said he thought that she was still in the main cabin with the others.

Kit stood, shaky on his feet, and went to the window. It was glassless and about nine inches square. Impossible to squeeze through. Beyond it Kit could see the stern of one of the keelboats still lashed to the *Zenith*'s side. From its windows yellow shafts of light danced across the inky water. "I suppose the door is locked?"

"Tight as a drum," Stromberg said.

"And there are at least two men guarding it," Gray Feather added. "We hear them talking from time to time."

Kit pressed his ear against the door, but all he could hear was wild whooping and carousing coming from the shore. "The Blackfeet are celebrating, and from the sound of it, they're rip-roaring drunk." He glanced at Gray Feather. "Wonder why Watkin separated the five of us out."

Hamner spoke up. "That's plain enough. It was you, Mr. Gray Feather, and the captain who embarrassed Watkin the most the other day. And as for me and Joe, well, it's the two of us he'd need most if he wanted to run this boat."

Kit tried the door. It didn't budge. He put an eye to the keyhole and saw only darkness beyond. "We got to get out of here," he said, pacing back to the window.

"There is no way out, Kit," Gray Feather told him. "We've already tried."

Kit looked at Stromberg. "This is your boat. Is there no way?"

"I'm afraid Mr. Smith is correct. Except through that door, there is no other way out of here."

Kit peered out the window again. He could stick his arm out of it, but that was all. Their freedom was so tantalizingly close, yet so impossibly far away as long as that door remained locked!

"I'll be back shortly," Watkin said, taking Charlotte as far as the door to the cabin on the *River Maid*. He opened it for her. Beyond lay a short, steep flight of steps that ended in a long, narrow room—similar to the main cabin on the *Zenith* but much smaller. The cabin was cluttered with crates and barrels stacked along its sides. A table dominated the center of the floor, flanked by three chairs. At the far end of the cabin was a cot with a pillow and rumpled blanket. There were four windows that looked out on either side, covered in dingy burlap curtains. Overhead hung an oil lamp and upon the table burned two thick candles in tin sconces. In spite of these, the cabin seemed a sinister and foreboding place.

"Make yourself at home," he said.

Charlotte ducked her head under the low doorway and went cautiously down the stairs. The ceiling was so low that she could barely stand up. None of the men would be able to stand straight in this place. A shudder gripped her slender form as the door closed behind her and she heard the sound of a latch being bolted softly. She reached into her handbag for a handkerchief and patted her eyes.

What am I to do? she wondered, moving along

the cabin. *How long before that wretched man returns?*

Resolve taking the place of her initial fear, Charlotte knew she had to do something . . . but what? She had to find a weapon!

She was sure she had several minutes at least before the river pirate returned, and she was determined to make the best of them. The first place Charlotte turned to was a stack of crates on the right-hand side of the room. Lifting a lid, she discovered them filled with old rifles. They were so badly rusted that she wondered if they still functioned. But unless she could find powder and ball, they would not be of any use to her. Besides, a rifle was just too awkward a weapon. There was no way to hide it. No, she needed something smaller, something that she could conceal. . . .

Quickly she lifted more lids. A knife was what she was looking for, but no knives presented themselves.

"Not even a rusty tomahawk, dammit!" she said aloud in frustration, glancing back at the junk stored within the cabin. There were plenty of colorful glass beads, some cheap cotton cloth, and a dozen or so kegs of whiskey, but no knives! Moving quickly in hopes of discovering something she had overlooked, Charlotte paused at a small crate filled with bottles. She lifted one. It was empty and mighty light, but the long neck made a convenient handle.

But if it lacks the heft it might not do the job. . . .

Charlotte patted her hand with the bottle thoughtfully. She was about to put it down and resume looking when an idea struck her. Inside the box was a tin funnel, and at once Charlotte knew out what the bottles were for. Quickly she yanked the cork, slipped the funnel into its neck, and struggled with a keg of whiskey. Happily, she discovered the bung had already been knocked in and a large cork stuffed into the hole. But when she grabbed the cork and twisted, it wouldn't budge.

She tried it again, but her strength was not equal to that of whoever had set the cork in the first place. Her nails clawed desperately at it. Then she heard footsteps outside. With renewed vigor Charlotte grappled at the cork, gritting her teeth and twisting with all her strength. It turned slightly, but that was enough encouragement for her to go after it with supreme effort. All at once, it popped free.

In a heartbeat she had tipped the keg over and was carefully spilling the whiskey into the bottle. Its *glub, glub, glub* sounded so loud to her that she feared it could be heard outside the cabin.

Another set of footsteps strode down the deck toward the bolted door.

The bottle was finally full.

Charlotte tipped the keg back, plugged the bunghole again, and immediately slapped the cork back into the neck of her bottle.

The latch rattled.

She bolted to her handbag on the table and was just slipping the bottle inside it when the door opened.

Watkin peered inside and smiled his artificial smile at Charlotte. It made her skin crawl. "Are you comfortable?"

Charlotte was seated at the table and tried to

look relaxed and resigned to her fate, but her heart was pounding her ribs.

She had just barely had time to race to the chair and arrange herself before Watkin's head had appeared through the doorway.

"I would be more comfortable back on the *Zenith* with my father," she replied curtly.

"You'll get over that," he said, latching the door before coming down the steps. At the table he showed her the bottle of whiskey that he had till then kept hidden behind his back. "This is the good stuff. Genuine Kentucky rye, aged . . . oh, at least six months. Not like this watered-down swill that we trade to the savages," he added, indicating the kegs stacked along one wall.

"I don't drink whiskey."

"I do." He yanked the cork and reached into a cubbyhole for two battered tin cups. "This is good stuff, really. Try it. You might find that you like it. If nothing else, a couple stiff swigs will help relax you."

Charlotte remained stiffly in the chair.

"Believe me, the night will be much more pleasant if you relax, my dear."

Charlotte shrugged her shoulders, conceding the finality of her fate, and set her handbag on the table. "Oh, why not. Fill it up," she said, pushing the tin cup toward the bottle.

With a glint of victory in his eyes, Watkin poured a generous portion into each cup. He raised his cup to her as if making a toast and tossed back a healthy swig of the liquor. The biting liquid wrinkled his face. He shook his head and smacked his lips in appreciation.

Hesitantly, Charlotte put the cup to her lips and pretended to take a long swallow.

Watkin came up behind her and put a rough hand on her neck.

"Not too fast," she said meekly. "Before I make love to a man, I at least like to get to know him a little."

His fingers tightened into her neck. Then all at once they released her and Watkin took one of the chairs. "All right," he said impatiently. "We've got all night. What is it you want to know about me?"

"Well, where are you from?"

"Virginia. But I left there for Missouri when I was twelve."

"By yourself?"

"It's not that unusual."

"Have you always worked the river?"

He laughed. "No, before the river I spent years on the stage." His voice deepened dramatically. He put his hand to his heart and flung it toward the ceiling. "I was a tragedian, my dear lady. No one ever played Oedipus with as much feeling as I! I should have performed on the stage of the Rose Theater in London, not Lacey Stegner's Riverfront Playhouse."

She feigned a laugh at his impromptu monologue and pretended to take another sip of the whiskey. "That explains it."

"Explains what?"

"Your line about me being more lovely than a summer's day, and all."

Watkin grinned. "I have learned that a well-placed compliment here and there takes some of the bumps out of the road of life."

"Why did you leave the stage?"

"Actors, my dear, are always hungry. I got tired of wondering where I was going to find the money for a meal or a pint of ale."

"So you became a river pirate instead."

His smile never wavered, but Charlotte saw his face harden ever so slightly. The truth apparently did not sit well with Watkin. "I'm a businessman," he said brusquely, "and I don't go hungry anymore."

"I'm sorry. I didn't mean to—"

"Never mind. We've done enough talking." He threw back the rest of his drink and stood. Unbridled passion smoldered in his eyes as he hovered over her.

Charlotte's blood ran cold. She took a sip from her cup—this time for real—and placed it ever so slowly on the table. She had held Watkin off with talk as long as she could. There would be no more stalling the man.

Suddenly he grabbed her by the arms and lifted her from the chair. He forced his lips upon hers. His rough kiss burned with such ardor, she could barely breathe. Charlotte was aware of his hands moving, roving, and she cringed as within her there arose only vile revulsion.

Chapter Ten

"Please, wait," she said breathlessly, managing to break from his kiss and turn her face to the side. "Not like this. Please allow me the dignity at least of undressing myself."

Watkin's panting breath burned against her cheek. "All right. But make it quick." He released her and began unbuttoning his shirt.

Charlotte said, "While I'm getting ready, why don't you straighten up that cot? If we are going to do this, at least we can do it right." As she spoke, her hand reached casually for the handbag sitting on the table.

Watkin grinned. "See, I told you you'd come around."

"I think I'm even looking forward to it," she said, feigning shameless lust.

He turned. Swiftly Charlotte's fist wrapped

about the neck of the bottle hidden in her handbag. She pulled it out and swung it into the back of Watkin's head.

It connected with a gratifying *thump* and the pirate lurched forward, sprawling flat upon the floor. Charlotte combed a thread of auburn hair from her eyes, breathing hard.

"Come around, you say? Not likely, Mr. Watkin!"

She knelt by the fallen man and put her fingers to his neck. She was relieved to feel a pulse. She had hit him with all her might, not daring to do any less, but she hadn't really wanted to kill him. Only stop him for a while—a good long while, she hoped.

"You are so right, we have done enough talking." Her knuckles had blanched around the neck of the bottle. She set it down and immediately drew the pistol from Watkin's belt. This pirate was out of the picture for the moment, but his keelboat still swarmed with others. Worrying that someone might try to peek in past the curtains that covered the windows, Charlotte hurried to the table and blew out the candles. She turned the wick of the lantern down to a faint glow. The room fell into deep shadows. Charlotte hoped the cutthroats topside feared their captain enough to not risk having their faces seem pressed against the windowpane.

She dragged Watkin to the cot, where he'd be less likely to be spotted, and left him lying on the floor beside it. Feeling in his pockets, Charlotte found the key that he had put there after locking Captain Stromberg away. Now all she had to do was get away from there and free the captain and the others.

The difficulty of accomplishing that crashed in upon her like a falling roof. How would she ever sneak past the men up on deck? Tightening her grip on the pistol, Charlotte climbed the three steps to the door and pressed an ear against it. At first she heard nothing. Then there came a soft cough, and a moment later some footsteps. Two men spoke in low voices, but Charlotte could not make out what was said. By far the most noise came from the nearby shore where the Blackfeet were whooping it up.

Charlotte thought about her father, held captive by those reveling Indians. What if they took it into their drunken heads to scalp him, just for the fun of it? She had heard such lurid stories about the natives of this land that she was convinced anything was possible.

She dared not linger any longer. What if someone knocked and Watkin didn't answer? Her time was short. Listening again, she heard the footsteps move around to the left side of the boat. Moving to the windows on that side, Charlotte glimpsed two shadowy men strolling along the deck toward the bow. A minute later she saw them pass by the right side of the boat.

They were making rounds!

She pressed against the door again, casting a fearful glance at the body near the cot. How long would it be before Watkin regained consciousness?

The footsteps stopped by the door, but this time they did not move off right away.

What are they waiting for?

Perhaps it was too quiet for them? Gathering up her skirts and dashing back to the cot, Charlotte gave a long, loud laugh and said, "Oh, Captain Watkin. You are so clever!"

There. Maybe that will satisfy them.

Back at the door she heard the men outside chuckle. "Lucky devil," one of them said. The other replied, "We'll all get our turn before Watkin gets rid of her."

"Oh, you think so?" Charlotte whispered to herself, resolutely hooking a thumb over the hammer spur of her pistol. "Just come on and try something with me, buster!"

The footsteps moved off. If she had it figured right, she'd have at least two minutes before they came back around. Silently she lifted the latch and slid it back. The door opened a fraction, creaking softly. Charlotte held her breath and waited. The stern of the boat remained silent. Pushing the door open half a foot, she stuck her head outside. No one was there. She crouched outside, kneeling so as not to be seen above the low roof of the cabin. It was now or never. With the pistol ready, Charlotte dashed to the stern, where the big rudder stuck straight out. A glance told her she'd made it unseen so far.

Suddenly she heard a laugh, followed immediately by a belch. It sounded so near that at first she thought it was right beside her. A man was coming back from the bow. Charlotte swung a leg over the stern and began to lower herself to the water. Her skirt caught on a belaying pin.

"Damn!" She was stuck halfway between the deck and the water. The man came into full view, and he would have seen her at once if his head had not been tilted toward the starry sky with a bottle of whiskey turned up to his mouth. Charlotte gave a yank. The skirt ripped. She lowered herself into the river as quickly and as quietly as she could.

"Say, what was that?"

"What was what?" another man answered from farther away.

"Did you hear something?" the first man asked.

"Didn't hear nothing but you belching and stinking up the air, McKinzie."

"Hmm. I could have sworn."

His heavy boot steps angled for the stern. Standing waist-deep in the river, Charlotte flattened up against the boat. To her consternation, she suddenly realized that the river had buoyed up her skirts, which now spread across the water like a wide pink and white water flower! Frantically she pulled them in and bunched them around her waist. Another man joined the first.

"What are you looking at, McKinzie?"

"Thought I saw somethin'."

"Ha! The only thing you've seen the last hour is the bottom of that bottle."

Charlotte hardly dared to breathe.

"Ah, maybe you're right."

"Getting skittish?"

"Naw. I just can't wait to have my turn at that gal. I hope Watkin don't use her all up before I get my chance."

The men chuckled and strolled off.

Charlotte let loose a long, pent-up breath, then she eyed the riverboat moored alongside them. Luckily, none of the pirates aboard the *Zenith* happened to be in sight or they surely would have spotted her. By now her skirts had been weighed down by the water. She eased herself toward the bigger boat, the muddy river bottom giving way beneath her at each step.

She would be in plain view of anyone aboard the keelboat until she got around to the back of the *Zenith*'s paddle box, and that could spell disaster at any moment. Lowering herself deeper into the water until only her head and the pistol were above it, Charlotte started aft, urged along by the Missouri's swift current. She moved as fast as she dared, fearful of tripping and wetting the powder in the gun. The paddle box rose up alongside her. A few seconds later she stepped behind its towering mass.

She had made it! Standing, she leaned against the paddle box, exhausted from the ordeal, relishing the deep shadows and the absolute impossibility of being spotted here.

For the first time since the pirates had taken over the riverboat, Charlotte felt a moment of safety.

Then something moved in the darkness.

Charlotte wheeled about, her heart beating wildly, the pistol ready in her hands.

A man-shaped figure emerged from the shadows and lunged at her. He moved faster than she, and before she could find the trigger or even cry out, a strong arm locked about her waist and a hand covered her mouth and dragged her back.

In the gloomy darkness of the boiler closet, only a hint of gray moonlight made its way through the tiny window. Kit sat atop a spool of rope and pondered their predicament. His head still throbbed.

He tried to ignore that. Every now and again Captain Stromberg would let out a small groan of pain, but for the most part everyone was quiet, mulling over their own thoughts, listening to the muffled conversation coming from beyond the locked door.

Looking at it from every angle, Kit knew that escape was impossible. They could do nothing until Watkin opened that door.

Sitting there, Kit became aware of an odd, rolling movement that hadn't been present a few minutes before.

"You feel that, Captain?"

"What?"

"We seem to be moving."

"We aren't, Mr. Carson. It's only the river rocking us."

"I know. But for the longest time we were planted on the mud as solid as an old oak tree."

"The river has chewed away the mud beneath the keel, is all. We are no longer stuck on that bar, but floating free. Just the same, Watkin tied us off to the shore, so we aren't going anywhere."

"No, but if someone were to cut that rope . . ." Kit suggested.

"Then we would be carried downriver," Stromberg noted, "until some snag or another bar stopped us. What have you got in mind, Mr. Carson?"

"I'm not sure yet. Just an idea."

Gray Feather said, "An idea that isn't worth the powder to blow it away unless we can free ourselves from this room."

"Amen." Hamner sighed.

"Maybe," LaBarge added, "but since we ain't going nowhere right yet, I'd like to hear what you got in mind, Mr. Carson."

"Miss Heath!"

It had been immediately obvious upon encircling her with his arm and having caught a handful of breast in the process that this was no river pirate or Indian warrior! It was a woman! He immediately released her.

"Who are you?" she stammered. In the blackness behind the paddle box Charlotte couldn't see a thing.

"It's me, Warren Randle."

"Mr. Randle? That's impossible. You're dead! I saw them shoot you!"

"N–no, not dead," he said, shivering. "But I'm beginning to wish I was. I'm about frozen! I've been in this water for over an hour."

"How did you survive it?"

"Wh–when I saw their intentions, I dove underwater. Their bullets only made it a few feet then they just sort of drifted down on me. I couldn't see a th–thing in the muddy water, but I just knew that if I stood up again I would be a dead man. Somehow, I swam a few feet and the current carried me along. The next thing I knew I had bum–bumped into the paddle wheel, and when I stood, I was inside the box. I didn't dare leave it. I waited until nightfall, thinking I'd slip out and try to make my way to safety. That's when I saw you. I couldn't see who it was in the dark. I thought you might be an Injun; figured to strangle you and hope to get a knife or tomahawk." He hesitated, obviously embarrassed. "Er, s–sorry I grabbed you like I done, Miss Heath."

"Forget it. I'm just glad you're alive."

"Wh–what's going on up there?"

"I don't know. Watkin took me off the boat shortly after they tossed you overboard. The crew and wounded were still in the main cabin, under guard. I have to assume they're still there. I have a bad feeling about them, Mr. Randle. Watkin was going to have them killed—he may still do so. The captain and some of the others, including that trapper and his Indian friend, are locked away in a room near the boilers."

"It looks hopeless, Miss Heath. Maybe we ought to just sneak away in the darkness while we still can."

"And leave the others to Watkin? Never."

"Maybe you're right. But what can we do?"

Charlotte thought a moment, then said, "Most of the men in the main cabin are wounded. The few crewmen there are seeing to their needs. Besides, they are too heavily guarded for just the two of us."

"That leaves the captain and the men with him."

Charlotte nodded. "If anyone can go up against Watkin and his cutthroats, it's that trapper, Mr. Carson. He's got grit. You can see it in his eyes. That man is tougher than old boot leather."

"I agree, Miss Heath. What do we do next?"

"Make our way back aboard the *Zenith* and somehow distract the guards by the door. I've got the key."

"How did you manage that?"

"It's a long story. I'll tell you later. We need to get this done before Watkin wakes up."

"Wakes up?"

Charlotte grinned in the darkness. "He made the

mistake of turning his back on a lady."

They waded out of the shadows. At the riverboat's stern Randle hoisted Charlotte high enough for her to grab one of the guardrails. She dragged herself heavily aboard, her soaked skirts weighing her down. Reaching back, she gave Randle a hand up. He crawled aboard and the two of them pressed up against a dark wall, dripping a spreading puddle of water at their feet.

"Come on," Charlotte whispered, leading the way forward, clinging to the shadows wherever possible. The keelboats tied alongside were bustling with activity as the pirates moved cargo around and made room for the American Fur Company stores that they had taken aboard. Charlotte and Randle slipped silently from one patch of deep darkness to another until they reached the boat's furnaces. The iron doors hung open and a red, flickering light spilled out from the banks of coal, slowly dying, softly illuminating the piles of firewood stacked up around them.

"There," Charlotte breathed near his ear, pointing at the two men lounging leisurely upon the handrail. The glow from the bowl of a pipe clenched in the teeth of one of the pirates showed his bearded face. The two guards were watching the shore, and the Indians there. From her vantage point, Charlotte could see that most of the Blackfeet were lying around in a stuporous state. Some appeared to have passed out. Others staggered aimlessly along the dark shore. She worried about her father's safety. The Indians had permitted their fires to burn low, probably because they were too drunk to have noticed.

"I will go forward and work my way in front of them," Charlotte said.

"What do you want me to do?"

She heard the trepidation in Randle's voice. Grabbing up a length of firewood, Charlotte thrust it into his hand. "I'm going to draw their attention. When I do, you come up behind and whack the hell out of them. Understand?"

"Miss Heath!" he said, shocked by her bluntness.

"Think you can do it?"

"Yes, I think so," Randle said.

His timorous reply was not reassuring. Charlotte glanced at the pistol in her fist. If nothing else, she'd do it herself if it came to it. "Be ready to move when I get their attention."

Charlotte worked her way forward. The bow of the boat was abandoned. Overhead, light from the main cabin made the front of the boat a dangerous place to be. She stepped quickly under the staircase, moving across to the port side of the boat, and stopped at the corner. Swallowing back her fear, Charlotte squared her shoulders, stood straight, put her arms behind her to hide the pistol, and stepped out into plain sight of the two guards by the locked door.

Chapter Eleven

"Whal, thar you have it," Kit said as he finished explaining what he had in mind. The only hole in his plan, of course, was that they were still locked up in that closet. And with two guards outside, and a half-dozen pirates prowling the riverboat's decks, the likelihood of breaking their way out of there seemed slim indeed.

"It would work," LaBarge replied, and the others nodded in agreement.

Captain Stromberg said, "Beyond the obvious problems, there would be the matter of overpowering the pirates still aboard the *Zenith*."

"I've crept into Indian camps to take back stolen horses, and I even managed to get inside the tepee of a sleeping Flathead chief once, Captain," Kit said. "If I can do that, I reckon I can come up behind a couple of half-drunk river boys and take them down."

"All right," Gray Feather said, "granted, we can cut this boat free, let her drift on the current while we build a head of steam, then make a run past the keelboats. We might even make it a few dozen feet before one of the pirates notices that we're no longer tied up alongside them. But tell me, how do you propose we break out of this closet?"

Kit frowned. "We can sit here making all the fancy plans we want to, but until we figure out how to jump that fence, we're just spitting in the wind."

The five of them fell into silence, glumly pondering their predicament.

A sound outside turned each of their heads toward the dark door.

"Say, what's this all about?" asked a wary voice from beyond the door.

"Ain't you supposed to be with Captain Watkin?" the second guard asked, puzzled.

Thump! Something fell.

A man cried out.

Thunk! Something else hit the deck.

The rattle of a key being inserted into the lock brought Kit to his feet, his fists rock-hard and ready for whatever came through.

The door opened.

"Captain Stromberg?" Charlotte's voice whispered. Her pretty face peeked inside.

They had dragged the two unconscious guards into the closet, relocked the door, and were now huddled in the shadows behind the furnaces. Kit glanced at the pistol that Charlotte held tightly by the barrel. "You're right handy with that, ma'am," he said.

"I've gotten in some practice this evening, Mr. Carson, and Mr. Randle helped too." She nodded at the rotund clerk, who was still clutching his club.

"That solves the first part of our problem, Kit," Gray Feather noted, encouraged.

Kit had appropriated a butcher knife and a brace of pistols from one of the pirates. "I'll see what I can do to whittle down the odds some."

Stromberg said, "Mr. Hamner and I shall rebuild the fires. Mr. LaBarge, you make your way up to the pilothouse. Once we are out in the stream, do what you can to keep us off any more bars."

"It won't be easy, Captain. Steering the *Zenith* with no power will be a little like trying to turn a buffalo stampede with a popgun."

"Do what you can. That's all any of us can do."

"I'll go with you, Kit," Gray Feather said. "Between the two of us we'll make short order of these rapscallions!"

They were about to take off in different directions when Charlotte said, "Wait! What about my father?"

"What about your father?" Kit asked.

"The Indians have taken him. Watkin told them that if I didn't cooperate, they could scalp him! We can't leave yet."

The men glanced at each other. Stromberg was the first to speak. "Hmm. That puts a different light on things."

"I knew it was going too easy," Gray Feather grumped soberly.

"Whal, reckon all we can do is go and fetch him back here, then." Kit looked across the dark water at the low fires burning on the shore.

"I'll go too," LaBarge offered. "I've had some experience with Indians."

They decided that Kit, Gray Feather, and Joseph LaBarge would go ashore to rescue Jerome Heath. Meanwhile, Stromberg, Hamner, Randle, and Charlotte would quietly begin stoking the furnaces. With any luck, they would still be able to carry out their plan.

The three men slipped quietly over the *Zenith*'s stern and, holding their weapons high, waded ashore, where they crouched among a stand of dark cottonwood trees. The lights from the riverboat and keelboats tied up at shore danced upon the rippling water. Overhead, dark shapes flitted through the air—bats taking their fill of the mosquitoes that plagued this river. From the Indian camp just ahead, drunken chanting and sporadic laughter filtered down to them.

Kit led the way to the edge of the trees, where they flattened out and studied the camp. There had been three big fires, but now two of them had burned down to embers. Around the third one sat seven men, passing a buffalo horn of whiskey between them. One of the kegs from the ship's stores was nearby, ensuring that the horn would not run dry anytime soon. If they just waited long enough, the entire war party would be out cold, but Charlotte had told Kit how she had escaped and there was no telling when Watkin would regain consciousness, or when his partners might find him knocked out. There was no time to wait for good ol' John Barleycorn to have his way with these Blackfeet.

Kit pointed out a pile of booty taken from the prisoners. "We'll find our rifles and pistols thar, I reckon. Think you can snake your way over thar, Joseph?"

"Reckon I can, Kit." LaBarge got to his hands and knees and started quietly off in that direction.

Kit had already spied Jerome Heath. The artist was sitting against the steep riverbank, hands and feet bound, and a sleepy-eyed buck sitting guard. Between Kit and Heath were half a dozen Indians. Some appeared asleep. Two of them were playing a button game with a basket and a pair of plum-stone dice. One glazed-eyed warrior stared vacantly out at the dancing lights as if mesmerized by them. It would take all the skill Kit had to make his way unseen through the intervening brush to cut the man free.

"Kit," Gray Feather whispered, pointing to a picket line where the Indians' horses had been tied. "There's my pony. And your horse, too. I can get them back for us."

This was no country for a man to find himself on foot if it could be helped. Kit said, "You'll never get those animals back aboard the *Zenith* without being seen."

Gray Feather considered this a moment. "I will take them upriver a couple miles and wait for the steamer to catch up. And when I take our horses, I'll scatter the other animals too."

"Now, thar's an idea. Getting them horses all rounded up again would give the Blackfeet something to think about. It would take their minds off of the riverboat."

"Or helping out Watkin any more."

Kit grinned. "The way I see it, all liquored up like they are now, they're already past helping anybody for at least a full day."

Kit and Gray Feather moved off in different directions. Gray Feather made a wide loop back behind the picketed horses. Kit sidled up to the steep bank, where he lost sight of both his Ute partner and Joseph LaBarge. With any luck, LaBarge would be gathering up their weapons now and very soon making his way back to the boat. Kit put the two men out of his thoughts. They were each on their own now, and each would have to do his best.

Nearby a Blackfoot lay curled up in his blanket. Kit drew the pistol and turned it over. He crept up behind the Indian, but the soft snoring and the aroma of whiskey that filled the air told him that this man had already fallen victim to the heavy drinking. Kit crawled off, keeping clear of the two gamesters tossing their dice into the air and catching them in their basket.

There was little cover on the exposed beach, but the lights on the water tended to make the shadows below the bluffs even blacker. Kit inched up closer to the guard sitting near Jerome Heath. The Indian had a rifle across his knees, a horn of whiskey in his fist, and sat sipping and watching the river. He never heard Kit come up behind him, and probably never felt the sudden rap of the pistol butt upon his head. Kit clamped a hand over the man's mouth to stifle any warning cries and lowered him to the ground.

"Kit!" Jerome whispered in relief.

"Hush!"

Kit dragged the Blackfoot back up against the rise and propped him up to make it appeared he was merely napping. Coming back, Kit sliced the ropes on Heath's hands and feet.

"My daughter?"

"She was all right when I left her."

"Then she is free of that man?"

"Worked it all out herself. You've got a feisty gal thar, Heath."

"Thank God she's safe."

"Whal, I wouldn't go so far as to say that—at least not yet. We still have to get ourselves clear of those pirates."

The two gamblers, not more than twenty feet off, were laughing and placing bets, rattling the stone dice loudly in the woven basket. Another of the Blackfeet had succumbed to the force of gravity—and whiskey—and was sprawled out on his blanket.

"Got to move quietly," Kit said.

"I'll do my best," Jerome replied, rubbing the circulation back into his wrists.

"Just think of the ground as a basket full of goose eggs. The point being, you don't want to break even one of them."

"I'll keep that in mind."

Kit led Heath back to the trees with little trouble. He was beginning to suspect that a man could almost wander freely through the Blackfoot encampment. Partying and revelry had made the warriors careless. But then, there was really nothing in particular that this band of Indians had to be on the watch for; they were in their own country and among their pirate friends. So, without much trouble, Kit brought Heath to the safety of the cottonwood trees, where he met LaBarge coming back from his foray.

"Got 'em, Kit," LaBarge said, placing the armload of rifles, pistols, hunting bags, and tomahawks on the ground. Kit recovered his weapons, and Gray Feather's too. LaBarge and Heath each took a rifle.

LaBarge checked to be sure that his was loaded. "I saw your friend, Kit. He clobbered a drunken guard, then cut the horses loose and walked them all away as if there wasn't a hostile Injun within a hundred miles of here."

"That would be Gray Feather's way," Kit said, relieved to hear that the Ute had accomplished his mission. "We'll pick him up along the river north of here . . . that is, if we can get away like we planned."

"Let's not waste any more time jawing about it," LaBarge said.

They stole away, slipped in to the dark water, and waded back to the riverboat.

"Father!" Charlotte cried softly as the two embraced.

"Are you all right?"

"Yes."

He hugged her tightly.

"How you doing here, Captain?" Kit asked.

Stromberg pointed at the pressure gauge. "Luckily, we didn't have to start with cold boilers. It's up to thirty pounds of pressure. We can turn the engines over anytime now, but we won't have full power until we build up the pressure to about ninety pounds."

Kit frowned. "Keep in mind that those boilers are full of mud."

"I could hardly forget that, Mr. Carson," Stromberg replied. "Where is Mr. Smith?"

"He scattered thar horses and took our mounts upriver. We'll meet him there and take him aboard."

"Very well. We will keep an eye out for him. Mr. LaBarge, to the wheelhouse."

"Aye, Captain."

Kit drew his knife. "Whal, reckon it's time I cut us loose of those keelboats. Keep your fingers crossed and hope we can drift out into the river before someone sounds the alarm."

Kit knew he was looking for a small miracle as he started for the *Warrior*'s stern rope.

"Been mighty quiet in there," McKinzie noted, eyeing the closed door to the keelboat's cabin suspiciously.

Baker Roland, a beanpole of a man with a deep scar down his left cheek, shifted the rifle in his arm and narrowed an eye at McKinzie. "You want to be the one to interrupt the captain? Not me, I can tell you that. You saw how he done in Copp. Cold-blooded, that man is."

"I don't want to interrupt nothing. I just want to know why it's so blasted quiet in there. Haven't heard a peep out of that girl for most of an hour."

Roland shrugged his narrow shoulders. "Maybe he went and killed her."

"He wouldn't do that . . . not yet, at least."

Roland scratched his stubbly chin. "What could go wrong?"

"Nothing, I suppose. Only," he glanced at the door again, "there should be *some* noise coming from there."

"Now that you mention it, it is unusual for them to be so quiet. At least you'd expect to hear talking now and then."

McKinzie went to the door and pondered his next move. Then he knocked. Unexpectedly, the door swung inward at his tap. Hardly any light escaped from the widening gap. McKinzie cast a questioning glance at his partner.

"Captain Watkin?" he whispered cautiously.

The interior of the cabin remained silent.

"Captain?" McKinzie called more loudly.

Nothing.

He pushed the door wider. The dim light revealed only an empty room. Then McKinzie spied the form of a man lying on the floor.

"Roland! The captain's hurt." Both men rushed inside.

"He's got a lump on his head as big as an egg!" McKinzie declared.

"I'll get a bucket of water." Roland plunged outside, and when he returned, four of the pirates came with him. He splashed the bucket over their leader.

Watkin groaned.

"Captain?" McKinzie said, helping the man to the cot. "What happened?"

Watkin blinked and looked around as if he didn't know where he was. Then his eyes cleared, narrowing suddenly in anger. "The girl?"

"She's not here. She was gone when we found you."

"The bitch knocked me out!" Watkin tried to stand. He staggered, and caught himself. "The riverboat! She must have gone to set the others free! Find her!"

Chapter Twelve

Carefully working his way forward, Kit froze at the sound of approaching footsteps. He stepped back into the shadow of a doorway beneath the boiler deck just as one of the pirates came around the corner. In a few seconds he would be at the boilers and discover the captain and others stoking them up.

Kit shoved the knife back under his belt and took his rifle in both hands. As the man walked past, Kit stepped out behind him and cracked him soundly on the head, then caught him by the shirt a moment before the blow could send him into the river. He dragged the man beneath the boiler deck and waited to see if anyone had heard him.

No one had.

Kit slipped out from cover and, crouching low, scrambled toward the larboard fender where the

Warrior's stern line was tied off. He began sawing away at it. The rope parted beneath his knife, and almost at once the keelboat drifted away from the *Zenith*'s side, still held against the current, however, by its bowline. To reach it meant that Kit had to cross the riverboat's prow where men aboard both keelboats would easily see him.

As it turned out, that problem dissolved into nothing when someone from the *River Maid* exploded from the keelboat's cabin with a cry that roused both crews to action.

"The girl escaped!" the pirate shouted. "Search the riverboat!"

With that rallying cry, the opportunity for quietly drifting away with the current instantly vanished. Throwing stealth to the wind, Kit dove for the *Warrior*'s bowline and slashed it in two. Instantly the moving river grabbed the keelboat in its mighty fist. It carried it downstream, swinging it about in the current and shoving it into the shore, where the boat stopped, canted crazily to one side.

Men scrambled to keep from being catapulted overboard. Crates and barrels that hadn't been lashed down spilled into the river. Two men tottering on her gunwales pitched forward and followed the cargo into the dark water.

Kit wheeled around, searching in the dark for the main line that held the *Zenith* to shore. He spied the heavy rope attached to the bow just forward of the broken jackstaff. By now men from the *River Maid* were streaming aboard.

Kit sprinted for the line. His purpose was plain enough to the pirates who immediately spotted him; like a school of sharks, they moved to cut him off.

Leaping atop the capstan to keep from their clutches, Kit rammed the barrel of his rifle into the chest of the nearest man, driving him back into the arms of two of his friends. A pistol cracked nearby, and hot lead singed Kit's forearm. He windmilled his rifle, momentarily keeping the pirates at bay as he cast about for a means to escape this hornet's nest. The mooring line that he had wanted to cut lay but ten feet away, but with the pirates swarming upon him from all sides, it might just as well have been ten miles. There was no way to get to it.

The broken jackstaff's foremost end lay back against the railing of the second deck. Seeing it was his only avenue of escape, Kit made a hasty leap, mounted it, and teetered there a moment as he fought to regain his balance. One step ahead of the pirates, he clambered up the pole, barely escaping their grasp. He grabbed the handrail and swung over it onto the promenade.

The pirates rushed for the stairs.

Another shot rang out, but this time it came from below, where Captain Stromberg and the others were attempting to bring the engines to life again.

Kit kicked open the door to the main cabin and burst through it. Inside, the two guards whom Watkin had assigned to keep watch over the prisoners were wavering between remaining there and joining their comrades outside. At Kit's sudden appearance their attention shifted away from the prisoners to him, and almost as if the whole thing had been planned, three of the crewmen who had been tending the wounded sprang for them. A rifle discharged into the ceiling, hurting no one. In a moment it was all over, and suddenly the pirates found themselves the prisoners.

Kit slammed the door shut behind him and wedged the back of a chair against its knob.

"That ain't gonna keep them pirates for long," Marcus Williams said.

"I don't expect it will," Kit replied, breathing hard to catch his breath. "But maybe it'll slow them varmints down long enough for me to figure out what I'm going to do with them next."

They flinched when a bullet crashed through the door and shattered the chimney of a lamp on the table.

"Is thar a back way out?"

"Follow me," one of the crewmen said.

"What about these pirates?" Marcus asked.

Kit briefly considered the problem and came to a decision. The pounding at the door told them that they had not an instant to waste. "If we leave them here that'll just be two more we'll have to fight later. Take them with us."

"Why not give them what they deserve?"

"Because we can put them to some good use." Kit was loath to leave the wounded behind, and here might be a way to get them out. "We can't leave these wounded men to those river dogs. They'll cut their throats for sure now." Leveling his buffalo gun on the nearest pirate, Kit said, "You and your pard pick up a man, and be gentle about it or I'll blow a hole in your gut big enough to float one of them keelboats through."

The big bore of the rifle before them was convincing enough, and the pirates did as they were asked without question.

Door hinges began to groan under the pressure of the pounding men outside. Kit drew a pistol and fired a shot into the door. A man beyond it gave a sudden cry. "That ought to give them something to think about," he said, shoving the gun back under his belt.

Kit urged them toward the back of the boat. The walking wounded were helped along by the hale and hearty, while the three more seriously hurt were borne by the two pirates and Marcus.

As if in reply to Kit's shot, four bullet holes suddenly riddled the door, driving the men inside the cabin to the floorboards. One of the pirates was a mite slow, and he gave a sudden grunt and lurched into a pool of his own blood. The man he had been helping crashed with him. Neither man moved afterward. Kit crawled over, grimacing upon seeing the scarlet hole in the wounded man's chest. There was nothing Kit could do for him now, and he still had the others to think about.

"Quick, before they can reload," he shouted, leaping to his feet. The trapper rushed the back door and flung it wide onto a vacant section of the promenade. The escapees piled out, and Kit swung the door shut behind them and barricaded it with a deck chair. For the moment they were alone, but it would not remain that way very long. From all parts of the boat came sporadic gunfire, the shouts of men, and the pounding of boots upon the deck below. A quick glance to the west showed that the Blackfeet had been drawn to the shore to watch the spectacle, but to Kit's relief it appeared that none of the Indians was in any condition to join in the fight.

He was worried about Charlotte and the others, somewhere down below, and he hoped that Stromberg and his men could hold out a little longer against the river pirates. Kit could have used Gray Feather's help just then, but the Ute was probably already a mile up the river with their horses. The battle had gone sour and their plans of a quiet departure had fallen to ruin. But maybe there was still a chance to get the wounded to safety before the pirates completely overran them.

Kit spied a ladder that led to the main deck. At the moment there were no pirates near it. "Get these men down to the river and ashore," Kit shouted above the explosion of gunfire that had just erupted within the main cabin. The pirates had made it through the first door, and it was only a matter of seconds before this second door burst wide open.

"What about you?" Marcus asked.

"I'll do what I can to give you enough time. Now, be moving quick, we ain't got but a few seconds."

"And him?" one of the *Zenith*'s crewmen asked, jerking a thumb over his shoulder at the one remaining pirate.

"I'll take care of the varmint."

"You'll be a dead man," Marcus warned.

"And so will all of you if you don't strike for that river right now! Get your hides moving!"

Reluctantly, the men gathered up their wounded friends and hustled down the ladder. Kit watched until they had slipped over the gunwale into the shallow water and had started for shore. The door bulged and the jamb began to crack. Kit shifted the muzzle of his rifle onto the remaining pirate, nudging him across the deck to the starboard railing.

"Up!"

"Up?"

"Get your mangy hide up on that thar railing, mister," Kit growled.

The pirate balanced himself on it, grabbing hold of one of the upright supports of the roof overhead. Behind Kit, the door splintered and groaned.

"Now make like a jackrabbit and jump. I want to see a great big splash at least twenty feet out thar in that river, and I don't want to see your head bob to the surface for at least thirty seconds. If I do I'm going to use it for shooting practice." The threat was all smoke and Kit knew it, for he didn't have thirty seconds to spare, but he hoped it might make this river rat think twice about swimming back to the steamer. He pressed the rifle into the man's back, and that was all the encouragement he needed. The pirate sprang out over the black water and disappeared.

Kit swung back around just as the door burst open. The first man through brandished a pistol, and upon spotting Kit he stopped and leveled the weapon. But Kit was a hairbreadth faster at the trigger. The big buffalo gun boomed and its thirty-two-gauge ball crushed the river pirate's sternum, passed on through him, and shattered the shoulder of the man standing behind him. Both lurched backward into the cabin and went down together as more pirates scrambled over them.

Kit wheeled his rifle to keep them back and batted aside a second pistol. One of the pirates leaped for the flying rifle and managed to grapple it away from him. They pressed Kit back into the railing. He snatched the tomahawk from his belt and sank its sharp edge deep into his forearm of the nearest man. With a howl of agony, the wounded man fell back, only to be replaced by another. But the odds were overwhelming. In a moment they had swarmed over Kit, grabbing for his arms, his hair, his legs. Kit swung out, catching another man with the short ax and hearing his scream. Then he went down. Something smashed into his head and fountains of colorful light burst before his eyes.

Kit tried to rise against their weight and was crushed back to the deck, his breath squeezed from him by the weight of the men piling on top of him. The tomahawk was torn from his fingers and his arms wrenched back until they felt as though they were about to be ripped from his shoulder sockets. Starbursts exploded in his brain from a second blow, and then he blacked out.

Icy water filled his nose, his mouth, startling him back to consciousness. His first thought was that he'd been thrown into the river, but as the fog lifted from his brain Kit's surroundings came into an uncertain focus, sharpening slowly with the return of his senses. He tried to move but could not. His arms ached and his shoulders burned. When he came fully awake, he saw the pirate standing before him holding a dripping bucket of water. From somewhere behind him he felt intense heat.

"He's awake, Capt'n," the river rat growled, stepping aside as Watkin came into Kit's view.

Kit groaned and discovered that he was swaying

oddly from side to side. His shoulders were ablaze with pain—pain he was beginning to feel farther up his arms as well. Something seemed to be cutting into his wrists, and he wondered briefly about the curious angle the deck seemed to be tilting. Then he realized the truth. The boat wasn't tilting. *He* was tilting! Kit dragged his feet under him and stood up all the way, instantly relieving some of the pain in his shoulders. He rolled his head back and blinked upward. His hands had been tied together over his head and his body hoisted partway up off the deck. That explained the pain in his shoulders and wrists. Kit had no idea how long he'd been suspended like this, but it couldn't have been very long.

Watkin planted his fists upon his waist and glared at Kit. "I told you I'd make you pay for putting your nose in my business, Carson. You'd have been dead already, except I wanted you fully awake to savor what I have in store for you."

"You're a horrid man!" Charlotte's voice rang out from nearby. Kit glanced over his shoulder and saw that Charlotte and the crewmen who'd been stoking the furnaces were under the pirates' guns. To Kit's right the yawning doors of the steamer's furnaces were wide open and two men were busily feeding wood into them. That explained the heat he was feeling.

"And as for you, my dear," Watkin hissed, narrowing an eye at Charlotte, "you could have made this so much easier on yourself." Watkin massaged the back of his head and winced as if he'd touched a particularly tender spot. "But because of your bad behavior, your fate will be the same as Carson's!"

"Please let her go," Jerome Heath pleaded.

"I have already given her one chance. I will not give a second."

"You can't be such a heartless bastard!" Heath shot back, his anger welling up.

One of the pirates cracked Heath across the mouth with a pistol, and he staggered, falling to his knees.

Captain Stromberg, holding his wounded arm tight against his side, said in a low, even voice, "Someday the law will catch up with you for this, Watkin."

"I doubt it. Who will know? None of you will ever tell. And my Blackfeet friends aren't about to report me to white authorities, either. They like their whiskey too much, and I'm their main supplier." Watkin laughed and returned his attention to Kit. "By the way, where's that Indian friend of yours?"

Even if it was too late to save himself and the others, the last thing Kit wanted to do was put Watkin onto Gray Feather's trail. "I don't know. Reckon he must have taken a bullet, or he'd be here now."

"Too bad. I had special plans for him, too. Well, it doesn't matter." Watkin dismissed the matter with a wave of his hand. "Hawk, bring the girl."

Hawk Marcetti hauled Charlotte to Kit's side.

"Throw a rope over that beam and tie her to it," Watkin ordered.

Kit noticed for the first time that the rope which held his wrists was actually attached to a boom of sorts, the variety used to lift and move heavy freight or equipment from place to place. In this case, its purpose appeared to be to swing out over the starboard deck and lift cargo—or perhaps machine parts—from a dock and deposit them near the boat's boilers. Marcetti bound Charlotte's wrists and tossed the end of the rope over the boom, making it fast.

"No, don't," Jeremy Heath implored as Watkin turned a hand crank, raising the boom, and with it Kit and Charlotte, until both swung back to back, half a foot free of the floor.

Watkin laughed. "Now for some fun. I hope you like the heat, Carson, because my men are stoking those furnaces just for you and lovely Miss Charlotte."

Dangling there, his back to hers, Kit felt the sudden rise in temperature as the boom was swung inboard as far as it would go. Watkin surely would have hung them full upon the glowing iron skin of the boiler if he could have. Fortunately, a timber that supported the overhead boiler deck intervened and brought the boom to a stop a mere foot and a half from the hot iron.

"Now," Watkin said, "let's see how long it takes before the corn starts to popping." As he spoke he gently massaged the back of his head again. "It's too bad it had to come to this, my dear. We could have put on such a performance, you and I. We'd have brought the curtains down and the audience to their feet!"

"You're a sick man," Charlotte said.

He grinned. "And you are about to be a roast duck."

Stromberg said, "Watkin, please. For the love of God, don't do this!"

"Hawk, the next time the captain speaks, cut his throat."

Hawk Marcetti drew the Arkansas Toothpick from his belt and grinned in anticipation as he tested the needle-sharp point with a tip of his finger. "What was that you was saying, Captain?"

Stromberg glared at the long knife and shut his mouth.

Kit felt the heat begin to penetrate his buckskin shirt and britches, warming his skin. Charlotte's clothes were much thinner than his rugged mountain garb, and he knew that she'd be feeling the heat even more than he. Kit tried to rotate himself between the furnaces and the girl to act as a shield, but he had little success.

The pirates had gathered near the boilers, and the deck was crowded with men looking on, wondering how long Kit and Charlotte could last while the captain, Jerome, and the rest of the crew stared helplessly on.

Nearby was a pile of their weapons, including Kit's rifle and pistol, but the pirates were armed to the teeth. No man could reach that pile and live.

Kit's shirt burned hotter against his skin. Sweat pricked his forehead and started trickling into his eyes. From behind him, Charlotte gave a soft groan. When he craned his neck around he was startled to see that Charlotte's dress, which was still wet, had begun to steam.

"Try to think of something else," he offered. The advice was lame at best, but it was all he had to give. A cool night breeze that had begun to blow steadily from the north did little to abate the intense glowing heat just eighteen inches from them.

"I'm trying to," she gasped, "but it's not very helpful."

Kit tried again to swing his body between Charlotte and the firebox, and again he merely swung back to where he had started. His shirt was becoming unbearably hot while Charlotte's low whimpering was becoming distressingly louder. And there was nothing he could do to help her.

Nothing!

Chapter Thirteen

After about five minutes, Gray Feather drew rein and sat astride his saddleless horse, a vaguely puzzled smirk creasing his shadowed face. He looked over his shoulder. Nothing moved back there upon the pale, moonlit prairie grass. Nothing moved anywhere, except for the dark, darting shapes of bats flitting overhead. He strained to hear any sounds of pursuit, which he was certain should be growing louder now. Instead he heard only the pawing and snorting of his and Kit's horse, the occasional buzz of a mosquito in his ear, and the sonorous croaks of a bullfrog chorus down by the river accompanied by the lively chirping of crickets.

As he relaxed, Gray Feather's smirk blossomed into a broad grin and he said aloud, "Those drunken skunks probably don't even know their horses are missing!" He shook his head, amazed. "And some folks have the audacity to say that no good ever comes of drink."

For mysterious reasons that he would freely admit he did not understand, Indians seemed particularly susceptible to "devil drink." He had learned all about intoxicating spirits a year or so after moving back east with his father when, to his misfortune, he discovered a bottle of Scotch whiskey in his father's liquor cabinet. A tentative sip, followed by a bolder second sip, and then another, culminated in a rip-roaring drunkeness, which was followed by a rip-roaring headache. That first time was also his last. Gray Feather had learned a valuable lesson, and he strictly avoided overindulging in the white man's "fire water" ever since.

He recalled that horrible experience now and laughed. "What am I doing running from ghosts—drunken ghosts, at that!"

Sighting a rise of land along the river to the east, he clucked softly and got his pony moving again, holding him to a walk. He climbed the rise to a high point where he could see the distant flicker of firelight from the Blackfeet's campsite. He could see the dark forms out on the water, but from this distance the riverboat and its keelboat remoras were impossible to distinguish from each other.

Minutes passed; the wait began to gnaw at his gut. If all went as planned, the steamer should be quietly drifting away from the other boats about now. But if things went badly, how would he know? He had told Kit that he would wait upriver for them, but now, considering the perils involved in the escape, Gray Feather began to question the plan. The escape had been a long shot at best, and it could be a short trip to a watery grave at worst.

His gnawing worry churned and churned, grow -ing steadily into a deep, foreboding concern . . . yet all he could do was wait. He briefly considered riding back to check up on his friend—the Blackfeet in their drunken state could cause him no trouble—but he didn't even have a gun or knife to help out if he should discover his friend in trouble.

No, Gray Feather told himself resolutely. *I said I would wait for the riverboat, and wait I will.*

He had just convinced himself that sitting tight right there was the best course to take when suddenly a pistol shot echoed up the dark waterway—then another, and another, and finally a whole storm of shots erupted down the river.

Gray Feather's spirits instantly crashed.

Kit's long shot had obviously gone terribly wide of the mark!

Hell's hot breath licked at Kit's neck and cheeks, and was turning his clothes into something worse than the hottest mustard plaster he had ever known. Charlotte's groaning had risen to a wail, and Kit would have gladly taken twice the heat to give her but a few moments respite from the sweltering inferno half an arm's length away.

Nearby, Jerome Heath was watching with open horror. But the poor father was unable to help his suffering daughter. The pirates had clubbed him to the deck each time he had attempted to rise to her aid. They kept him there under their guns, forcing him and the others to witness the slow deaths.

Licking his lips and tasting bitter salt, Kit said, "Watkin! Cut Charlotte down. Take your wrath out on me if you must, but spare the girl."

"Spare the girl? What a noble gesture, Carson. I commend you. But I'm afraid it cannot be." He gestured to the pirates feeding wood into the blazing furnaces. "Stoke them higher, mates."

Kit blinked the moisture from his eyes and caught a glimpse of Captain Stromberg. The captain's wide eyes were fixed not on them, but on the boilers. Kit blinked again, but immediately his eyes filled with the streaming sweat. A part of his brain wondered about Stromberg's distracted fascination with the boilers, but a much greater part of it was consumed with shutting down nerve endings and trying to shunt the pain of slowly roasting skin.

Finally Charlotte could stand the heat no longer and cried out. Spurred by her agony, Jerome lurched forward, only to be pounced upon by two burly pirates.

Watkin laughed. "I see that you do not like watching the fruit of your loins shriveling like a prune?"

"You're a monster!" Jerome raged.

"Indeed. You have yet to see what a monster I can be."

"Watkin!"

The river pirate turned back. "What? Another plea for mercy from the noble Mr. Carson?"

His skin felt as if it were blistering and his mouth had become dry as old leather. The initial pain of the ropes cutting into his wrists had long since paled compared to the fiery heat of the *Zenith*'s furnaces. Kit had to find a way to get to this man, to anger him to the point of rashness. But Watkin was not the sort of man to take rash actions. Still, there had to be a way.

"Mercy?" Kit forced a laugh. "I reckon not. Thar's likely more virtue to be found in a hungry grizzly b'ar than in a cowardly river rat who would torture women."

"Mighty bold talk for a man in your straits, Carson."

"Bold talk don't shine when it comes to knives and tomahawks, Watkin. But then, what would you know of such things? It's only cowards who take advantage of the fairer sex. If you was even half a man, you'd cut these ropes and put a knife in this child's hands. Then you and me can end this in a proper fashion—if you got the nerve. 'Course, I feel obliged to warn you that I was raised by a grizzly b'ar and thar's painter blood filling my veins. I eat river riffraff for breakfast and spit out their bones. Then again, thinking it over, a fellow ill-bred like yourself probably wouldn't take to an honest challenge. 'Course, if you don't, every man here will know you for the coward you are. If you're worried that I'll jump boat, you can forget that. Your pards will see to it that I don't run off."

Watkin peered at Kit a long moment, then laughed. "That was eloquent! My dear Mr. Carson, you have missed your calling. You would be superb as Macbeth, or Antonio! But I am afraid I must decline you colorful challenge. I much prefer to watch the two of you suffer slowly than to give you the pleasure of dying like a man."

Watkin was not a man easily swayed by words. Kit had tried and failed. He looked away and rolled back his head, feeling sweat stream down his neck, desperately searching for another ploy. Charlotte's crying had stopped, and he wondered if she had passed out.

Stromberg cleared his throat.

Watkin said, "Yes, Captain? You wish to say something?"

Kit shifted his view back in time to see Stromberg give Hawk Marcetti a sideways glance. Watkin said, "Oh, I see your concern. Well, I give you permission to speak. Hawk will not slit your throat . . . this time. Will you, Hawk?"

The pirate reluctantly lowered his foot-long knife.

Stromberg said, "I feel compelled to warn you that you are building a dangerous head of steam in the boilers."

"I am?" Watkin studied the machinery a moment. "Then perhaps we ought to vent some of it off. Hmm, let's see. Ah, this lever here. It opens the steam cocks, does it not?"

"It does not. That lever sends the steam to the engines," Hamner advised.

"The engines? This is what makes the paddles turn?"

Stromberg nodded his head.

Watkin reached for it.

"No!" Stromberg gasped.

"It frightens you?"

Stromberg calmed himself and said evenly, "Pulling that lever might prove disastrous. When the engines begin to turn they will pump cold water into those hot boilers. It can very well cause an explosion. You need to let the fire burn down first."

"Ah, I see your game now, Captain. You think you can trick me into ending this drama by telling me that there's a pending danger. Well, I'm afraid it won't work. More wood into those fireboxes!" Watkin ordered.

At that moment the sound of a falling crate crashing to the deck came from the stern.

"What was that?" Watkin said, wheeling about. The men listened, but the night grew quiet once again. Watkin turned to two of the pirates and said, "Go see what that noise was."

The men dashed toward a ladder, for the only way past the two paddle boxes to the stern was up and across the third deck where the pilothouse sat.

"Maybe it fell on its own," Hawk suggested.

"Perhaps." But Watkin wasn't so sure.

Kit's head felt light and somehow detached as the pain of being roasted alive by the huge furnaces began to overwhelm him. A minute passed, then another. All at once another crate fell to the deck. This time the crash came from the bow of the boat.

Watkin called out the names of the men he had sent. When they did not answer, he ordered another pair of pirates to the bow to investigate. He paced across the deck and shot a sharp glance at the captives held there. "Something is up," he said finally, directing his stare at Stromberg. "Who else is aboard this boat?"

Stromberg shook his head. "Far as I know, we're the only ones left."

Watkin's gaze moved past Randle, LaBarge,

Hamner, and down to Jerome, who was still on the deck, held there by a boot in his back. He turned and shot a glance at Kit.

"Some of the prisoners got away before we were able to catch Carson," one of the pirates said. "They slipped overboard and made their way to shore before we could stop them."

Watkin wheeled and strode to the larboard-side railing. He peered across the water to the gathering of Blackfeet on that shore.

Something splashed quietly near the *Zenith*'s starboard side. Kit blinked several times to clear his eyes. When he was finally able to see, his spirits shot up like a skyrocket. Gray Feather was pulling himself up out of the water onto the deck! Immediately the Ute disappeared into the deeper shadows behind the boilers. With adrenaline coursing though his blood, Kit felt his vitality return and the pain throughout his body temporarily subside.

Watkin and the others lingered upon the larboard side, searching the shoreline.

Like a phantom rising from the netherworld, Gray Feather was suddenly and silently at Kit's side. The feel of cold steel touched his burning skin and the ropes parted.

"Was that you making a racket?"

"It was," Gray Feather whispered. "And I collected these from our pirate friends when they came to investigate." He put a knife into Kit's hand, then he sliced through the bindings that held Charlotte with the second knife that he had appropriated.

They lowered her silently to the deck, where she

rolled her head and groaned, halfway between the conscious and unconscious world.

Kit's first thought was to slip overboard and make their way to safety, then figure out how he was going to rescue the remaining crew aboard the *Zenith*. But before he could put that plan into action, one of the pirates looked over.

"They're getting away!" the man cried.

"Get them!" Watkin shouted.

And the next thing Kit knew, a solid wall of river pirates were charging across the deck at them.

Chapter Fourteen

Although Kit had only been nine years old when his father, Lindsey Carson, had died, he still vividly remembers the long talks they would sometimes have in the evenings, after the chores were finished and the day spent. Lindsey would sit in his favorite chair on the porch of their two-story log home, his boots propped on the top railing, the red glow from the bowl of his pipe softly illuminating his rugged features. Mostly, Lindsey told stories of the war and such—he'd fought in both the War for Independence and the War of 1812—and oftentimes he would impart bits of wisdom that he saw fitting to hand down to his son.

"During General Jackson's war me and a couple of your brothers joined up with the militia and went to muster in at Fort Kinkead. We had us some close calls fighting the British and Injuns, but none so harrowing as a time I remember once when a bunch of us volunteers come upon a band of Creeks on the warpath. Them Injuns outnumbered us six to one, and some were even carrying British muskets! Me and my partners suddenly found ourselves in a real pickle barrel. What do you suppose we did?"

Kit remembered shaking his head. "Don't rightly know, Pa," he had replied, his eyes wide just thinking about meeting up with wild Indians on the warpath.

"Whal, son. We done exactly the opposite of what them Injuns expected. Why, any sensible man might think to turn and hotfoot it out of thar, but we was headstrong mountain boys. I said, 'Lay into 'em, brothers!' and we done just that. Fired our rifles and pistols empty and leaped to the challenge. Hollering like wild Injuns ourselves, our tomahawks and knives eager to taste blood, we showed them what to expect out of Americans. Routed the whole lot of 'em, we did, that afternoon. And other than Pete Crocker losing a piece of his nose, not one of us so much as got a scratch."

Lindsey then peered sternly at his son, and Kit had known that a lesson was coming. "Take a bit of learning at you pap's knee, Kit. If you ever find yourself with your tail up again' the wall and the back door closed, do something bold, something daring, something no one would expect of you."

Ever since then Kit had tried to live that lesson, even though some folks have on occasion pegged him as being a reckless sort for it. But so far it had held him in good stead, and Kit could see no reason to abandon the advice now.

Standing away from the gunwales, where a moment before he had entertained thoughts of jumping, Kit tightened his fist around the knife Gray Feather had given him, and giving forth a wild panther roar, he lowered his head and charged them all by himself. An instant before the inevitable clash, Kit clamped the knife in his teeth and leaped for a rafter overhead. Grabbing hold of it, he lifted his feet and his momentum carried him forward. Kicking out, Kit caught two pirates in the jaw, snapping their heads back with a resounding crunch of teeth and vertebrae. The momentum of his swing carried him on, punching a wide hole in their ranks. He dropped catlike to the deck behind them.

Taking advantage of the sudden confusion, John Hamner reached back into the shadows and came around with a stout belaying pin. He smashed the skull of one of the river rats who had been keeping them under guard, then turned to take on two more. Utter confusion broke out, with LaBarge and Randle each jumping into the fray, and Stromberg doing what he could with one wounded arm.

Watkin rallied the pirates and took the lead in the charge. He had murder in his eyes as he singled out the mountain man. Kit dove for the cellar and rolled under him, coming to a stop against the pile of weapons the pirates had confiscated from them. His rifle was there among the others, and he grabbed it, rotated, and shoved it up and crossways to block the downward swing of Hawk Marcetti's Arkansas Toothpick.

Marcetti's forearm cracked against the rifle's barrel, and the shrill cry of pain that burst from his throat was enough to set even the most seasoned field surgeon's nerves on end. Marcetti's fingers sprang open and the knife slipped from them. Instantly, Kit snapped the rifle upward, driving its butt into Marcetti's jaw with a bone-shattering crunch. Marcetti staggered back, opening the way for the man behind him to come through. Kit shot a foot and caught him squarely on the kneecap. Another unnatural snap resulted, and the second pirate went down with a squall of intense pain.

Rolling to his left, Kit barely avoided the butt of a rifle aimed at his nose. A roll back to his right, and the pirate that had leaped for his throat crashed headlong into the deck instead. Kit sprang to his feet, the heat of the battle completely eliminating the pain from the heat of the furnaces a few moments before. His rifle was not loaded, but it made a fine club, and in such close quarters with pirates and crewmen everywhere, no one would dare fire a pistol or rifle anyway.

Kit blocked a tomahawk blow and rounded, driving his rifle into the man's gut. As he buckled, Kit jerked up with the butt, destroying yet another man's eating hardware for life.

Something struck Kit across the back. He lunged forward with the breath knocked from him and his rifle clattering to the deck. Catching himself on one of the timber supports of the boiler deck overhead, Kit turned back to see Watkin standing there with a rifle in his hands. The rifle must have been empty, for Watkin promptly dropped it and drew a pistol.

In the melee behind Watkin the two crews battled with knives and clubs, but the pirates seemed to be regaining the upper hand.

"You have become the proverbial thorn in my side, Carson," Watkin growled, his narrowing eyes reflecting the red firelight from the open furnace doors like a monster from hell's infernal pit.

Kit drew in a painful breath, the bruised muscles across his back expanding as he straightened up. "You should have used that lead thrower on me the first time, Watkin." Kit stepped away from the timber and Watkin moved with him, keeping the pistol pointed at Kit's chest. "It was a mistake not to finish me off when you had the chance." As they circled, Kit moved closer to the knife that Hawk Marcetti had dropped. "You only have one shot, so you best not miss, 'cause I won't give you a second chance."

"I'll say it again, that's mighty bold talk for a man in your position, Carson. I have the gun, or haven't you noticed?"

Kit cast a glance at the others. Above the ruckus Gray Feather was yipping like a coyote, his slashing tomahawk glinting in the firelight as he fended off two men near the starboard-side fender. Randle was doing the best he could. Hamner and LaBarge were back to back, just barely holding their own. Stromberg was sprawled on the deck, unconscious . . . or dead. There was someone missing—Jerome Heath.

To Kit's dismay, the rowboat from the beached keelboat was just putting in to the *Zenith*'s gunwale, carrying in it the rest of the pirates who had been pitched into the river. In a moment reinforcements would be clambering aboard, but Kit couldn't think about that now. He had to keep his eyes on Watkin.

They had circled around, so Watkin's back was

toward the furnaces. The glare of the fires was nearly blinding. Kit kept one eye shut, an old backwoodsman trick to prevent complete night blindness when lighting a pipe of tobacco or approaching a stranger's campfire at night.

"You forget. I was raised by a grizzly b'ar and painter blood flows through my veins."

"So you have said. I think that perhaps it's time to take a look at some of that panther blood you've been boasting of." Watkin's finger curled around the trigger.

One of the pirates whom Gray Feather had been fighting suddenly pitched across the deck, clasping both hands to a bloody gash in his shoulder. Kit grabbed the man and yanked him around. The pistol boomed, and the impact of the bullet drove the pirate back into Kit's arms. He shoved him aside and dove for the Arkansas Toothpick. Snatching it up, Kit charged the river pirate. Watkin tried to bat the long knife aside with the pistol, but Kit had put all his weight behind the lunge and the blade drove deep into Watkin's belly. The force of it shoved the man back into the machinery, where he landed against the lever, cranking it all the way open. With the sound of rushing steam, the big boat shuddered.

Watkin stood there, wide eyes staring unbelieving at the hilt of the knife against his stomach. He opened his mouth to speak, but before a word could come out he slumped to the deck, dead.

The big paddles had commenced to turn, and with them the steam engines automatically started to pump cold river water into the overheated boilers. Hot iron began to crackle and squall. In a flash, Kit remembered Stromberg's warning when he had first boarded the *Zenith.*

When you hear them start to shriek like a banshee, that's the time to abandon ship without looking back.

"Gray Feather!" Kit roared, pausing only long enough to scoop his rifle off the deck. "Over the sides!"

Kit took two steps toward the boat's fender, then saw Stromberg move upon the deck. Without breaking stride, he grabbed the captain by the belt and heaved him over the gunwale into the river. Wheeling to his right, he brained one of the pirates still battling his Ute friend. Casting about, he saw that the crew of the *Zenith* had heard the screaming boilers too, and they knew exactly what it meant. The keelboat men were momentarily dumbfounded by the crew's sudden departure from the battle scene and their mad scramble for open water.

"Jump!" he told Gray Feather, giving him a shove.

Kit's view fell upon Charlotte. She was sitting on the deck, looking confused, with Jerome at her side, holding her in his arms. Kit sprang over a dead body and grabbed Jeremy by the shoulders.

"What?" he asked, dazed.

Kit heaved the startled man into the river, then, taking Charlotte around the waist under one arm, he leaped overboard. The river came only to his chest. When he hit bottom he plunged beneath the surface, dragging the struggling girl with him. A half-dozen powerful kicks brought them to deeper water, and then . . .

Hell burst wide open!

The volcanic roar was something akin to what

Kit imagined the coming of the end of the world might be like—like a hundred kegs of gunpowder exploding all at once. Even under the water it was ear-shattering. The Missouri River trembled all around him and its murky depths were suddenly as bright as daylight—an odd orangish daylight. The concussion of the exploding riverboat drove Charlotte and Kit flat onto the muddy river bottom as if they had been pounded by a giant fist; a mighty hand held them there while all around them bits and pieces of the boat began to rain down, some spearing deep into the river bottom. Kit had all he could do just to hold his breath and pray that none of the falling debris would crash down onto them.

The heavy hand finally lifted, but the deadly rain seemed to go on forever, until finally Kit could remain under water no longer. Drawing his knees up under him, he sprang to the surface, hauling the gasping and sputtering Charlotte Heath with him.

Overhead an eerily glowing orb of pumpkin-colored steam was shooting skyward, spreading rapidly out across the river, and from within it splintered wood tumbled back to earth. Where the riverboat had once been, only a few timbers remained, thrust up out of the roiling water like the skeletal remains of some huge beast. Everything above the waterline had completely disappeared . . . including the pirates and Jimmy Watkin's keelboat, which had been lashed to the *Zenith*'s gunwale.

Slowly the deadly rain subsided. To Kit's amazement, he had managed to retain his hold on Charlotte Heath under one arm and still grip his rifle in the other hand. Stunned, his body numb and tingling all over from the fierceness of the explosion, his ears ringing as if a million bees were swarming inside his head, Kit waded through the flotsam toward the shore.

Peaking above the horizon, the fiery morning sun reminded Kit all too vividly of the riverboat's glowing furnaces and all that had happened only a few hours earlier. Kit had not slept that night. After helping rescue the men who had leaped or had been tossed overboard, and after tending to the wounded, Kit had gone off by himself to contemplate his own mortality—something he rarely, if ever, did. But last night's close call reminded him that life was tenuous at best, and living out in these wild lands made it all that more fleeting. Just waking up in the morning was a toss of the dice!

Kit was grateful to be alive, and he drew in a long, exhilarating breath, casting off his gloomy mood as the land around him brightened with the coming of a new day. His clothes were still wet and clammy in the chill night air, and he longed for the coming warmth so he could dry out, and the coming light so he could more fully survey the wreckage that not long before had been a fine riverboat. Its gray remains were taking on color now.

There was not much left of her except some ribs sticking up out of the water and a piece of her stern with a scrap of the boiler deck still attached and twisted to one side. The shoreline was littered with bits and pieces of wood and iron for as far as Kit could see. He fancied that in a few months some of the *Zenith* would be arriving back in St.

Louis, the city of her birth, although he doubted if by that time anyone would recognize the scraps of timber for what they were—or had been.

"A penny for your thoughts?"

Kit turned. Charlotte Heath was pretty as ever, although her dress was ragged and she had a weary, threadbare cast to her face.

"Just thinking about life," Kit said.

"And what have you decided?"

Kit shrugged his shoulders. "That sometimes it don't seem to be worth very much. That a man best take the time to enjoy what years the Good Lord has given him, 'cause it only takes one slipup and thar you are, standing on the edge of eternity."

"My, you're in a philosophical mood this morning, Mr. Carson."

"Sorry. How are you feeling, ma'am?"

"Chilled. It is much warmer near the fire, though. I came to invite you over. You've been sitting here just staring for hours."

"I could use some coffee."

"I think everyone feels that way, but I'm afraid all of our food and coffee went down with the boat."

Kit stood and accompanied her to the fire.

"You're looking a mite flushed, ma'am."

She gave a short laugh. "I feel like I have lain out in the sun too long—in the altogether," she added impulsively, averting her eyes at so suggestive a statement.

Kit grinned. "Whal, least we can be thankful the Blackfeet vamoosed when the *Zenith* busted up." The Indians had fled the riverbank upon the boat's explosion, many of them feeling her scalding breath upon their naked skin. Drunk as they were, they must have figured that the white man's contrivances were something to keep at a great distance, thank you, and Kit was inclined to agree with them. *A sensible lot,* he mused to himself. "They're likely still running down the ponies that Gray Feather turned loose."

And the pirates were gone, too. Those who had survived—if any could have who were on board when the *Zenith* exploded—must have made their way to shore and taken off on foot.

Stromberg rose from his place by the fire, where eight or ten men were seated. His arm was bandaged and his head wrapped in a scrap of cloth where it had taken a sharp blow, but he looked to be in good condition. "Take my place and warm yourself," Stromberg offered.

"Thanks, Captain." Kit turned his hands to the fire to warm them, but he did not hold them there long. His skin was still tender from the ordeal at the furnaces. All around him sat the weary lot of survivors, tired and hungry men who were just grateful to be alive.

"What are you going to do now that you lost your boat?" Kit asked.

"I have signed a contract with the American Fur Company to deliver its goods to Fort Union. And that is exactly what I intend to do."

"Without a boat?"

"But you are mistaken. I still have a boat, Mr. Carson." Stromberg pointed downriver to where the *Warrior* had beached after Kit had cut her lines. "It may not be the boat I started with, but it will float. Did I mention that I'm an old keelboat man myself?"

"You did."

"She will do in a pinch. I've already been aboard her. She's sound and carrying a good portion of the cargo that Watkin and Smitter intended to steal. Randle is there now, making an inventory of what is left. I have enough men to make up a crew, so there you have it. We will rest up today and be on our way tomorrow." Stromberg cleared his throat. "And I gather that when we depart, you and Mr. Smith will not be accompanying us?"

Kit shook his head. "I've been to see the critter once, and once is enough for me. From here on out I think I'll do my traveling on foot or horseback. Horses don't blow up."

Stromberg chuckled. "I can understand your feelings on the matter, Mr. Carson. We are most fortunate that you and Mr. Smith happened along when you did." He drew in a long breath and snorted it out. "At least we are able to salvage something from these river pirates." His face grew somber with that thought. "But we lost a lot of good men in the fight."

They looked up at the sound of hoofbeats.

Gray Feather reined to a stop. "Our horses were right where I left them, Kit," he said. "There's so much green grass hereabouts that they had no need to wander off. Just stayed put filling themselves."

"Reckon we ought to ride off some of that fat. Wouldn't want them to get spoiled."

The Blackfeet had departed in such a hurry that they had left most of their booty behind, including Kit's and Gray Feather's saddles.

"Will you be leaving right away?" Charlotte asked, disappointment showing plainly on her face.

Kit was anxious to be on the move again, but he wanted to see Stromberg and the survivors safely back on the river before riding away. "Gray Feather and me will stick close by until you shove off in the morning. Everyone here looks hungrier than pilgrims. We'll go see if I can't hunt us up some deer meat."

Jerome Heath limped over and stood by his daughter's elbow. "I haven't had a chance to thank you for your help, Mr. Carson."

"No need to," Kit said. "Sorry that all your painting gear and picture work went down with the boat. And all your flower-collecting stuff too, ma'am."

Heath put an arm over Charlotte's shoulder. "All of that is replaceable, Mr. Carson. I am just grateful that I did not lose the one thing that is not." He gave his daughter a tender squeeze. "I have you to thank for that."

Jerome's maudlin words were nearly embarrassing and made Kit uncomfortable. "I only did what any man would have. Say," he exclaimed to change the subject, "I plum forgot. You wanted me to tell you all about Bridger."

"Bridger?" Jerome paused a moment, searching his memory, then nodded his head. "That's right. With all that happened to us I completely forgot about him." He made a wry smile. "As it turns out, we don't need to have that conversation any more."

Kit was puzzled.

Heath continued. "Jim Bridger is just a name that folks back east have heard of—a bigger-than-life legend that appears in newsprint from time to time. But these last couple days I've learned all I need to know about trappers and Rocky Mountain men. I have no need to chase legends anymore, for I've met the genuine article . . . Kit Carson!"

Now Kit was really embarrassed. His cheeks warmed, and he was at a loss for words. Luckily, Gray Feather was there to hurry him away under the pretense of a hunting excursion.